Solus

Solus

DON WILLIS

RESOURCE *Publications* · Eugene, Oregon

SOLUS

Resource Publications
An Imprint of Wipf and Stock Publishers
199 W. 8th Ave., Suite 3
Eugene, OR 97401

www.wipfandstock.com

PAPERBACK ISBN: 978-1-6667-6088-0
HARDCOVER ISBN: 978-1-6667-6089-7
EBOOK ISBN: 978-1-6667-6090-3

10/25/22

Contents

Part 1

BEN HAD WORKED AT the Center for Off-World Life and the Company for nearly thirty years and didn't like the acronym today any more than the day he helped found it more than two decades ago. Politicians loved acronyms, but he never knew, and no one had a good answer for why a government committee came up with COWL other than the fact that politicians don't like long titles, unless it is their own. Any person in Congress is happy to say that I am Congressperson so and so, the chairperson of the subcommittee on silly names and naming from the second district of such and such State, but for agencies they want to come up with acronyms so that they can assign us a title of no more than a syllable or two. Although it irritated him to no end, he lived with it, because those are the people he has to crawl to on a regular basis for the funding of his project, and his project was his whole world. After a lifetime of work, they were within days of flipping the switch and finally answering the question that humans had been asking since they first looked up at the stars. . . .. .are we alone?

Part 2

Fifty Years earlier

A NINE-YEAR OLD BEN was attending Church with his mother and father. Every Sunday morning, Sunday night, and Wednesday night, his parents, his brother, and his sister got into the family car and would head to Church. On rare occasions Ben would ask to skip Church, but he always knew the answer he would get from his dad. "If you think Jesus is ok with it, then it's ok with me." Everyone at Church knew them and they knew everyone. The kids would run around in the basement of the Church until it was time for Sunday School to start, then it was time to be in your seat and be quiet while one of the adults taught a kid-focused lesson from the Bible. After Sunday School it would be time to go upstairs where they would sing three songs, hear announcements, send around the offering plates, and then hear a sermon that was guaranteed to either put the children in the audience to sleep, or make them amazingly antsy in their seats. Hearing various parents say 'Shush' or 'Be quiet', 'Stop that', 'Sit down', or the best, 'Wait until we get home', was common fare every service. Ben was no exception. There was something comforting about the routine though. In the sixties and seventies, it was the time that everyone would be dressed in their finest suits or dresses to come and worship God, who most likely couldn't care less what you were wearing, just that you were doing good by him and your fellow travelers here on this blue ball we call

Earth. As much as he hated to admit it, Ben liked going to Church and seeing his school classmates in a setting other than school. It didn't hurt that Ben liked seeing the girls in their dresses as opposed to the pants they wore during the week at school. A lot of his male classmates didn't like girls when they were young boys, but Ben couldn't remember a time when he didn't think that girls were the most amazing of all of God's creations. At all ages, Ben could look at girl and think that she was more beautiful than any work of art, especially Susie. Susie was a fellow nine-year old, who not only went to Church with him, but was also in his class at school. Ben got in trouble more than once or a hundred times for staring at her. It was as if he stared at her long enough, the image of her would be permanently burned into his brain and he would never forget her. Approaching her though, or even speaking to her was an impossibility. Ben started kindergarten when he was four years old, so he had always been the youngest, and the smallest boy in class. Getting picked on and bullied were parts of his normal routine at school. Church was a nice break from the bullying. He got to spend time with kids his own age without wondering who was going to shove him, make fun of him, or punch him. At school, those fears were always in his head. It wasn't until his sophomore year in high school, that he had a growth spurt that got him close, but not quite to six feet tall. He also had put on some muscle mass, since he was on the wrestling team. As a result, the bullying had stopped, but in his head, he always felt like the timid, weak, bullied kid that was always one wrong word, look, or gesture away from getting pummeled again. It didn't matter what grade they were in at school, Susie was always the girl he dreamed of someday having the nerve to ask out on a date, or even speak with, even if it was just to say hello.

For Ben, being twelve was the year from hell. Early in the year he had lost both of his grandfathers. One to cancer and one to a heart attack. Later in that year, his parents, his brother, his sister, and both of his grandmothers were killed in an auto accident as they drove to a home and garden show in Indianapolis. The only reason he was alive is that he had been sick, and was left at home to spend the day in bed. In a single year, not even a year really, just a matter of about seven months, his entire family had been wiped out, and he was left alone in the world. The day that the police, along with child services pulled up to his house to tell him and take him away was a day that burned into his memory forever. There wasn't a moment, a detail, a smell, or a sound that he could ever forget about that day. Life had begun to pummel him just like the bullies he would encounter at school. To deal with the trauma of his loss and the fear he would face at school, he withdrew more and more into books. It didn't matter what kind of books. History, science, fiction, sports, any kind of book would do as long as he never had to raise his head above their pages. The world was cruel, and the people in it even crueler. But in his books, he could escape to places long ago, or places of fantasy. He could escape into history, or into equations of math and physics. He could escape into the microscopic world of cells, bacteria, and viruses. Over time, books became his friends and his family. They were the only ones that were always there for him. They never let him down. He kept every book he ever read, because family stays together, and his books were his family. To the outside world, he learned to develop a separate personality that he would wear like a mask when he went out in public. He had found, over time, that never looking above the pages of a book resulted in even more beatings from bullies, than being invisible. As a result, he studied different behaviors and found one that lessened the beatings. To the world he would appear outgoing, playing parts in various school plays, singing, being in band, and even some sports. He would joke around, and appear friendly, longing for the school bell to ring to signal the end of the day, when he could retreat into his books. Life in the foster system, was little better than being at school. The people in his home were more than willing to ignore him and let him keep his face buried in his books. They clothed him, fed him, and put a roof over his head, as the State paid them to do, but were fine with having nothing to do with him during his stay with them. His teachers at school didn't care for him either. He always knew the subject matter for his classes better than the teachers. He sailed through every class with ease, and routinely corrected his teachers when they got something wrong. As a senior, Ben took a college prep chemistry class. For his project he designed, this being 1979, an automobile engine that could run on hydrogen.

He got a C on the project because the chemistry teacher said no such engine could ever be designed, or ever work. Later in life, Ben would see the research being done to develop hydrogen engines for automobiles and a smile would come across his face when he saw the schematics. They looked nearly identical to the project he had turned in back in 1979. A part of him would have liked to have given his old chemistry teacher a phone call to see if he would like to correct the grade. If the teacher had still been alive that is.

By the time of Ben's graduation from high school, he had been in four different foster homes. He ignored every person in the homes he was in, and he liked it that they ignored him as well. His grades were never impressive, but it was not for lack of knowledge and intelligence. He would routinely argue with teachers and administrators about how pointless testing was, the way they conducted it, and therefore never cared about how he performed on those tests. Not a single test, either in high school or college, ever actually tested his intelligence on a particular topic. All tests ever did was test a person's ability to memorize and recite a set of facts for a length of time to cover the taking of the test. He always argued that if any of his teachers would like to actually test his knowledge of a subject, then they should engage him verbally. Anyone could recite that a particular battle took place on a particular day, but engaging the student verbally opened so many more possibilities to test the depth of their knowledge and understanding about the question. In an oral test, that allowed the student to expand their response, they could tell you that the battle took place on a Tuesday. The ground was wet from a mist that had blown in that morning. The young men on both sides were scared out of their minds. Some so terrified, that they ran, even at the risk of being shot as deserters. Some considered running, but the shame they would feel for having left the battle, and being branded a coward, kept them on the line to face almost certain death. The student could have expanded on the fact that many of the young men could taste the bitterness in their mouth from the amount of adrenaline pumping through their veins. The student could tell the teacher that they were shaking so badly from fear, that few of them would ever hit a single person, no matter how many times they fired their guns. The student could have expanded on the fact, that once hit, many of these young men would call out for their mothers, hoping that she could make them feel better, even though they lay dying. The student could expand on the fact that the battle would rage for days, yet when it was over, the battle line would only be moved a few feet, costing thousands of lives per inch gained or lost. The student could expand on how many families suffered because a son, husband, father, or brother was never coming home again and the hole that would be left in the lives of these families for decades to come. That is the true way to test knowledge and understanding. Filling in a circle for A, B, C, or D tests nothing other than luck or memorization. We test for short term knowledge that will be gone with the sunrise after the test is taken, and wonder why people have no long-term understanding of themselves or the world around them. Even as a senior in high school, he had come to realize that testing students had nothing to do with the testing of students. The people actually being tested were the teachers, administrators, and the schools. If the students did poorly, it was the schools that would be punished. Over the decades that passed to the present, that meant that schools continued to lower standards, lower the quality of education, and teach to the testing the students would take rather than to their educational advantage.

Today, the high school version of that would be behind him. Today he would be graduating from high school, and then heading to college, where he expected poor teaching and testing would start all over again. He dressed, ate lunch, grabbed his cap and gown, and drove to school. No one would be in the stands watching him take his diploma, shake the hand of the principal, or turn his tassel. He parked his car and walked in to the school. He walked down the hallway toward the area where all of the graduates were supposed to meet. On the wall of the hallway, he saw a poster. One of the Churches in town was hosting a party for all of the graduates. Every graduate was welcome, even if you didn't normally go to that Church. Ben had not darkened a door of a Church since his family was killed, and he had no intention of doing so now. His anger toward God for the death of his family, and his life since had gone from a visceral hatred, to simply a part of who he was. He had no clue how a loving God could heap so much sorrow on a child, and heartache and sorrow was all that he had known since the day that they died. On top of that, the poster reminded him how alone he was in the world. Through all of the school dances and proms, there had never been anyone on his arm, so he never attended any of them. Today, the day of his graduation, there was no one there to watch, no after graduation party to attend, and no friends with whom to celebrate. Once they tossed the hats in the air, he would be going back to his foster home, closing the door to his room, and reading another book. It was a life to which he had become accustomed. After they tossed their hats, he saw Susie in the hallway and actually worked up the courage and fortitude to say 'hi'. She turned to see who had spoken. Once she saw who it was, she nodded her head a bit, and then turned back to her friends and continued her conversation with them. He had loved her from afar since they were small children. That nod of the head was probably the most she had ever acknowledged his existence. He walked out of the school and saw groups of students heading to various parties. He continued alone back to his car, and drove back to his foster house. As he drove away, a small tear flowed down his cheek. On a day that was supposed to be a happy milestone in the life of a young person, he had never felt more alone, and that was saying something for him.

Part 3

Colleges turned out to be exactly what Ben expected. More people his age that ignored him, and that he ignored. More teachers who knew less about their subject matter than he did, and tests that tested short term memorization skills rather than long term understanding. It didn't take long for Ben to become a fixture at the various libraries around campus. The improvement, for him, over high school, was the libraries. He could spend all the time he wanted in them, other than his obligatory class attendance. He even slept in the libraries now and then. A twenty-four hour a day library was a dream come true for him. His particular fields of interest were physics, Astro-physics, chemistry, bio-chemistry, and pretty much anything to do with any scientific or engineering field. The additional option he appreciated was the chance to go to classes over the summer. He had no one to go home to, and nowhere he called home, so staying on campus was ideal. The one indulgence he allowed himself was to intern for a company that worked with NASA on various projects. He had been assigned to work with a PhD working on Astro-physics and for the first time, since the death of his family, was enjoying something. The head of the department had seen something in Ben that he felt should be cultivated. He provided Ben with books, research papers, studies, the latest data from various projects, etc. Ben soaked it all up like a sponge. Ben was consuming the information nearly as fast his boss could provide it. For the rest of his life, Ben would credit his boss for having learned more under his guidance, than in all of his college classes combined. Ben had little respect for any professor he ever had, or even the ones he didn't have. After obtaining his Bachelor's degree, he was invited to speak to a class of PhD candidates. Each one of them described their thesis to him and were each amazingly proud of their work. Ben was amazed, thinking they had little of which to be proud. Not a single thesis, held any commercial or scientific value. Ben spoke with the professor and the reason was obvious. The professor, now in his sixties, had gone straight from being a student to being a professor. He, like most other professors Ben had ever met, had no experience in the real world. They did nonsensical research, and published papers for the benefit of other nonsensical professors. Each nonsensical professor would read the work of another nonsensical professor and applaud their nonsensical work, so that other nonsensical professors would applaud their work. They would then take the praise obtained from other nonsensical professors to their various Deans and say 'look at the praise my nonsensical work is getting', in order to justify the money being wasted on their salaries. All the while these nonsensical professors were cranking out nonsensical degrees, from nonsensical universities, and the students paid the price by graduating with no usable knowledge or skills. The further along the university treadmill Ben trod, the less respect he had for the institution, which was something to say considering how little respect he had for it to begin with. If it weren't for the fact, that to get where he wanted in his career, he needed a PhD, he wouldn't be there. It was a lot of wasted money and a lot of wasted time.

There was one bright spot in his time at the university however and her name was Deanna. Ben had only ever loved one girl before and that was Susie. He had loved her since elementary school, but she barely knew he even existed. A head nod of acknowledgement and a humph, was about all he ever got from Susie. Deanna was intelligent, very pretty, and was the rare person who could make Ben look up from a book long enough to generate a conversation. Neither of them had any experience in romance, both being reserved, brainy people that kept to themselves. As a result, they both fell for each other quickly, and married within months of their first date. Their favorite activity to do together was read research papers. They would talk over this theory and that experiment, each in turn either defending it, or tearing it apart. They both loved science, and talking science with each other. After they both finished their Bachelor's degrees, they began working on their Master's and PhD's. It wasn't very long before Deanna was expecting their first child. It was the first thing, since before his family had died, that was bringing Ben out of his shell. He was excited about something other than science for the first time in a very long time. He and Deanna would pick out baby clothes, furniture, toys, and all of the accessories that go along with having a baby girl. Ben felt such a deep love for this little girl that he had not yet even seen. It was beyond him how someone he had never met could have such a hold on his heart. Ben had sketched out what she could look like, based on a combination of his and Dee's features. He would occaisionally talk to the sketch, professing his love for her and her mother, and talking about all of the things he would teach her, the places they would go, and all of the toys they would play with as she grew. He could not wait until the day he got to hold his little daughter in his arms. Every time he saw Deanna, she looked more and more beautiful to him. She would fret about the weight she was gaining, but all he saw was the most beautiful mother anyone had ever seen. He had a sense of peace and fulfillment that he had never known.

Shortly after she began to gain weight and get her baby bump, they got news from her doctor that the pregnancy was in trouble. She was classified as high risk. At the five-month mark, the doctor told them they may need to consider terminating the pregnancy. Both Deanna and Ben were devastated. Ben was willing to terminate. He could not imagine a life without Deanna. As excited as he was about having a daughter, a life without Deanna was beyond anything he could possibly bear. Deanna, however, was not willing to terminate. They did everything the doctor recommended to increase the chances of delivering a healthy baby. Deanna suspended her studies for her PhD, and began a life in bed to minimize the strain on her and the baby. At the six-and-a-half-month mark, Deanna began to go into labor. They rushed to the doctor, and by then her contractions were only a minute apart. The doctor checked her and she was only dilated by two centimeters. They attached the fetal monitor, and it showed that the baby was in a great deal of stress. The urge to push was overwhelming, but the doctor told Deanna that she couldn't. The doctor told the nurse to prep for an emergency C-section. They rushed Deanna into the operating room. For Ben, waiting in the hallway seemed like an eternity. It was way too early for the baby to be born. He worried about anything and everything that could be wrong. Preemie babies had a hard way to go and so many potential health risks. He just hoped beyond hope that they would both be alright. He even prayed. Praying was something he had not done since his family was killed when he was a child. Eventually a doctor came out to see him. She looked dejected. She touched Ben's shoulder. "I am so sorry." She said to him trying to console him. Ben looked at her with tears going down his cheeks. "Did we lose the baby?" He asked hoping the doctor would simply tell him that Deanna and the baby were having some sort of difficulty. The doctor's eyes were welling up as well. "We lost them both. I am so sorry." Ben dropped to his knees. He looked up at the doctor as if she had to be lying to him. This had to be the worst practical joke ever played. It wasn't possible. They had just been at home an hour or so ago, talking about room colors for the nursery. Ben stared at the doctor and leapt to his feet. "YOU'RE LYING! WHERE IS MY WIFE?!" He screamed through the tears as he struggled to comprehend that his wife and child were gone. His legs were like rubber. He was shaky, and the room seemed to be spinning. "I have to see her." He ran past the doctor and into the room where they had taken Deanna. There she was. The only part of her that he could see was her face. The rest of her was covered by surgical sheets. The doctor entered the room behind him. He walked over to her and put his hand on her cheek. He told her that she needed to wake up. He begged her to wake up. "Please Dee. Please don't leave me." He leaned over and kissed her cheek. He begged her over and over to wake up and not leave him. "What am I going to do without you Dee?" He looked up at the ceiling and let out what could only be described as a primal scream. There was so much sorrow in that sound. He just kept repeating No, no, no over and over again. "She can't be gone." He looked back at the doctor. Tears, like rivers, were flowing down his face. His speech was breathy and interrupted by the sobs cracking his voice. "Can't you defibrillate, or ventilate her, or something?" He walked over to the doctor. "Please bring her back." He got down on his knees in front of the doctor. His hands clasped together as if he was praying to her. "I'm begging you. Please. I can't go on without her." He got up and walked back to Deanna. The sobbing was almost guttural it was so intense. "Please don't leave me Dee." He fell back to his knees, with his hand holding hers and just cried.

Ben arrived back at their home. Their home. There was no 'their' anymore. He walked from room to room, remembering things he and Deanna did in each room or said to each other in each room. He couldn't stop the tears. He sat on the bed and sobbed, rocking back and forth, missing the woman he loved so dearly. He thought about what he would need to do in the next few days. He and Deanna had no family except for each other. Neither of them had any friends. Both of them had been lonely bookworms and science geeks that found each other, in a lonely world that had been so lonely for the both of them. They had never talked about burial arrangements. They were both so young, who thinks about that when you're in your twenties? He couldn't imagine burying her in a grave and having her embalmed body lying there for decades to come. The idea of it was creepy to him. To stand on the surface and imagine that a few feet down, the body of the person you love is still there. Day after day, year after year. It was a morbid thought to him. He liked the idea of natural burial, but he only liked the idea for himself. He couldn't bear the thought of bugs, worms, bacteria, and other organisms feeding on his Dee. Cremation seemed the only possibility, but what would he do with the ashes of Dee and their little girl? He didn't want to spread the ashes somewhere and them be lost to him forever. He didn't want to put their ashes at the base of a plant that he could keep. What if the plant died? It would be like he lost them all over again. After a lot of thought he finally settled on turning their ashes into a diamond. He would then have a ring made for the diamond and he would be able to keep them with him for the rest of his life. He couldn't sit still or rest. There was no way he was going to sleep. When he laid in the bed, he laid down on his side and just stared at Dee's side of the bed. He rubbed it and instead of tears, he was filled with rage and anger. His rage was not directed at Dee for leaving him. His rage was directed at God. He laid on his back looking up at the ceiling. "IT WASN'T ENOUGH THAT YOU TOOK MY FAMILY WHEN I WAS A KID? YOU HAD TO TAKE THIS ONE TOO?!?!?!?!" He pounded his fists beside him on the mattress. "WHY? WHY DID YOU DO IT AGAIN? ONCE WASN'T ENOUGH? ARE YOU THAT VINDICTIVE?" He kept repeating the word 'why' over and over again as the tears streamed from his eyes.

Part 4

THE NEXT FEW WEEKS were like going through the motions of a life. He retreated into his books, his studies, and his research. He was nearing completion of his PhD thesis. He was writing about an engineering design that would allow for the scanning for life in the entire Milky Way galaxy in a single scan and from our solar system. His professor didn't understand the science any more than his high school chemistry teacher understood his hydrogen car design. The professor spent the last several months questioning everything about the thesis, but after looking like a fool multiple times, he had stopped. Though his professor was far behind him as far as the science, the professor at least recognized that Ben was far beyond any teaching the professor could provide. His theories would take years to just work out the math, and then possibly decades to design and build the equipment necessary to prove the theories and do the scan. That was far into the future, and all he could think about was that it would be a future without his beloved Dee, and the daughter he would never see grow into an adult. No dressing up time, no tea parties, no first step, no first tooth, no first anything. It was simply back to Ben, as it had been for most of his life, and would be for the rest of his life.

The day he graduated with his PhD should have been a happy day. One of the advantages of this graduation versus his high school graduation was the option of not going. He simply had the university mail his diploma to him. He had no friends at school, and no one with whom to celebrate. The only person that would have mattered was gone, so the day of his graduation, he was at home reading research studies. Just prior to his graduation he had been approached by a company who had seen his thesis and wanted to fund his research. His one requirement was that he would be the head of the project and would only have staff when he reached the point of needing staff, and there would be no requirements for him to socialize as part of the job. They had agreed, and the day after graduation, he arrived to work, was shown where his office was located, where his lab would be when he was ready for it, and he got to work. They had offered a very generous compensation package. A generous salary, an apartment on the university campus where he would be working, ten percent of the profits from any patents he generated from his research, a substantial retirement plan, and complete medical, dental, and vision at their expense. It was the kind of deal he would have loved telling Dee about when he got home, but instead he had no one to tell, and no one that cared. The Company saw from his thesis how many inventions would have to come out of his research to make it work, and were more than happy to line up for the ATM that his research would become for their company. The Company had offered the university a large donation in exchange for allowing Ben to do his research there. If Deanna and their daughter were still here, he would have never agreed to housing on campus, but he requested it. There was nothing to go home to any longer, so the idea of living so near to his work was appealing. Nothing other than his work had any meaning to him any longer, so why not live within a stone's throw of work. He sometimes would go to his campus apartment to sleep, but more often he simply slept in his office. It was a large office, and he had requested a twin bed and a private bathroom with a shower, so there was almost no need for the apartment, but it was there and was sometimes a change of pace. At his apartment, he had an office set up, so he could work there as well as at his campus office. The two were quite interchangeable, and there was little to tell them apart except for location.

During the next few years on campus, he would meet with the board overseeing his project funding and update them on the status of the math he was working on, so that they could proceed to the development phase. Not a one of them understood the math or his theories, but that was to be expected. If they understood it, they would have no need of him and would simply take over his project. Occasionally, the Company would send him to this conference or that conference to have him speak. The Company was like a farmer showing off the prize pig at the fair, and that's often how he felt. He hated being in the presence of other people. It brought his anxieties to their highest levels. In front of a large crowd, he had no problem speaking, but one on one, he would be screaming for the nearest exit on the inside. He had no gift of small talk, so when he would be required to join a cocktail hour to wander the room and 'chat' with people, he would often grab a glass of soda from the bar, make sure the people from the Company saw that he had made his appearance, wander around the edge of the room for a length of time, and then head back to his hotel room. He had little use for other people, and would prefer to stay back at the university, in his office or apartment, and work.

After seven years of working out the math and formulas for all of the theories and the equipment that would need to be built, he was ready to move on to the development phase. Ben began working with the engineers to develop all of the equipment that would be needed to accomplish the task of scanning the entire galaxy in a matter of hours. It was no small task. Not a single piece of equipment needed for the task existed. It all had to be invented from scratch. Since Ben was the only one that could do the math or design the equipment, the Company had an enormous 'key man' insurance policy on him. As a result, the doctors from the insurance company knew every square inch of Ben's body very well. They oversaw his food intake to a large degree, although Ben often drew the line when he would tire of the tasteless garbage he often had to eat. He had come to a truce with them some years ago, by implementing 'cheat' days when he could eat whatever he damned well pleased, and let them control the other days. The upside to having a team of doctors dedicated to keeping you healthy is that you do stay very healthy. The downside, for Ben, was having no one to share this healthy life with any longer. There was hardly a day that went by, that he wouldn't dream of telling Dee about what he had done that day. And each year that went by, he imagined what their daughter would look like, and what her voice would have sounded like. So, he continued to work, and allow the work to consume his thoughts, because if he didn't, the loneliness would consume him instead. He preferred to work alone, but those days were now gone. He was now the head of a team of engineers and theorists from various disciplines. He had to direct equipment engineers, software engineers, coders, building engineers, rocket scientists, astrophysicists, and a host of people from NASA, that always thought they knew better than he did what was required for his project. No one could know what was better for his project, because none of it had ever been done before. All of them played their political games trying to put themselves into a position that would either garner them a portion of the glory if the project succeeded, or insulate them if it failed. Ben cared nothing for the politics, or getting credit, or attention. He simply loved the work. The people with whom he had to work to accomplish that, could have all the glory for all he cared. He just wanted them to be competent so that the project would succeed.

Part 5

THE NEXT TWENTY PLUS years were a whirlwind of activity. Thousands of patents had been filed, making the company and Ben obscenely wealthy. Ben still had little to show for it however. Even though he was the lead for thousands of employees scattered around the world, he still lived in his campus apartment. He cared nothing about the trappings of fortune or fame. The one indulgence he did allow himself, even though it was also at the insistence of the Company, was a personal assistant whose sole job was to take calls and requests from media folks and in polite fashion, decline their requests. He stressed the polite part, because the company made him promise to be polite to the media, even though he had no respect for them, or any desire to be respectful. The Company also had her check on him regularly. Ben had a tendency to forget things like showering, due to his obsession with his work. It brought about the typical complaints from board members, when Ben would update them on his progress at their meetings. Thankfully, after his assistant was hired, the offensive odors at the meetings stopped.

Over the last year or so, the pieces that would make up the collector, necessary to collect the energy required to power the scanning satellite, had been launched to take up its position between Venus and Mercury. A team of astronauts had to be sent with each launch to assemble their piece or pieces of the orbital collectors. There were still another three years of launches to complete the construction of the satellites. There were always at least three ships enroute to the satellites due to the travel time between the satellites and the Earth. Once construction was complete, there would be nearly two years of testing and simulations to run before powering up the collector. All the time the collector was being built, the scanning satellite was being constructed above the plane of our solar system, or below according to your perspective, since up or down have little meaning in space. This satellite was in direct line with the collector below it, and contained the scanning device. Likewise, it had multiple ships going to and from it during construction, and it too would be running tests and simulations for two years after construction was completed. With all of the travel to and from the satellites being constructed, that meant hundreds of astronauts pulled from countries around the globe. With three to four ships enroute to the satellites, and six astronauts per ship, that meant that at any one moment, there were up to forty-eight astronauts on their way to the satellites. That also meant there were up to forty-eight heading home from the satellites at any one moment. Considering that the trip took more than a year each way, and two months of installation, any one crew could be away from home for over three years for a single trip. With the time away from family and friends, the goal was never to use any one astronaut for more than a single mission. It wasn't always possible. Some of the skills necessary were simply present in far too few people to make that happen, but no one was ever forced to go. Thankfully, there were so many wanting to make the trip, that the limitation was training, and identifying the trainees with the necessary skill to do the job. Another key point they had to identify was the psychological. Living in tight quarters, and being in close proximity to the same five people for that length of time, it was a necessity to make the right teams. Creating a team of six that had the needed skills, wouldn't kill each other before they got back home, and could handle being away from everything and everyone they had ever known for that length of time was a task to say the least. Accomplishing that for a single team is difficult enough, but it had to be done for up to four teams per year, every year, until construction was completed. This had become an international project, with more than fifty countries involved in funding, working, and providing astronauts to see it through.

The schedule was on a tight deadline. In four years, the satellites would be in the perfect position to get the best result. That meant that by the time Ben was fifty-nine, they would have to be ready to activate the scan. If not, it would be another five years to wait for the right positioning, combined with the right solar activity to get the maximum results. Their schedule only had a one-year cushion in it, and with everything being done, and the testing needed to make sure it all worked correctly, one year was very little leeway. In the midst of these deadlines and timetables, the Company had set up a news interview for Ben, without his knowledge, or permission of course. Ben threw a fit when he heard about it, and he refused to go. After hearing from him about how tight the timeline was and the consequences of missing it, they reminded him that the project was well on track, the progress was well within tolerances, and that his objection was more about the fact that he simply hated doing interviews. He was reminded of his duty to the Company, the Board of Directors, the shareholders, the taxpayers, and all of the countries involved in the project. He was also reminded that the project had been going for multiple decades now, and an interview was not an unreasonable thing for them to request of him. Concluding he was getting nowhere, Ben relented and agreed to do the interview. The news company agreed to come to him, so at least it wouldn't be as time consuming as if he needed to travel somewhere. That night, he decided to go to his apartment to sleep, rather than sleep in his office. When he got home, he sat on his sofa, reached for his picture of Deanna, and began telling her about the idiots he would have to speak with tomorrow. He had no clue how he was going to dumb down his work so that a reporter would understand. He found reporters to be one level of understanding above an amoeba. Although he would rather spend time with the amoeba. Reporters were the ambulance chasers of the media world. They would make anyone's life a living misery if it meant they could get one more point in the ratings, or one more set of eyeballs on their website. He detested them, and tomorrow he would have to sit with one of them and make nice. After venting to Deanna for a time, he began to feel better. Talking to Dee, always made him feel better. How he wished she was still with him. She had been gone for nearly thirty years, and it felt as if she had gone away just yesterday. He was still waiting for the day when missing her would get easier, but it never came.

He opened his laptop, and pulled up a picture of their daughter. It wasn't actually their daughter, but some time ago, he had come across software that allowed him to take pictures of himself and Dee, and approximate what their child would look like. He knew it was a composite and not what she would actually look like, but it was all he had. Every year, on what would have been her birthday, he updated the photo by aging it one more year. She would have been in her twenties now. He imagined what her life might have been. Would she have gone to college, trade school, been in a rock band? He chuckled at that one. Neither Dee or Ben had any musical talent. Would she be married? Would he have grandchildren by now? He had missed so much of what could have been, with them both being taken from him so long ago. He stared at the photos of Dee and their daughter all night, until he fell asleep on the sofa.

The next morning, he awoke to the sound of the alarm from his phone. He got up, saw the note from his assistant reminding him to shower. He showered, got dressed, and headed to the office to get this pointless interview behind him so that he could get back to work. When he arrived, his assistant shoved a bagel at him and told him to eat it so that he wouldn't be cranky during the interview. Pointing out how cranky he got when he was hungry might make him cranky, and he gave her a sideways glance to let her know just that, as he inhaled the bagel. The crew put makeup on his face, and pointed to the chair in which he was to sit for the interview. The reporter introduced herself, reviewed the questions that she would ask, and told him to relax and to be natural. Ben smiled his I hate being here practice smile, but it was mainly because there was no way she would actually want Ben to be natural, or he would be letting her know what he thought about her profession. She let him know that this was being recorded, and was not live, so if they made a mistake, they would simply repeat it and do it again if needed, before editing out the errors. With that, the lights went up and the reporter began her opening words to the camera. She introduced herself and Ben, gave a synopsis of the project, and then began her questions. There ended up only being one question, and Ben's response to it was why. "Doctor Prentiss. What is it you hope to accomplish with this project?" He listened to the question and was dumbfounded. When she said she was going to ask it, he thought she was joking. It was such a moronic question. It reminded him of a video he had seen long ago, of a press conference where the doctor talked about the organs donated by a specific donor, and all the lives saved. A reporter then asked if they could speak to the donor. The doctor did his best to treat it like a serious question, but the 'are you an idiot' expression could not help but cross his face. The doctor replied, "That will not be possible. The donor donated his heart, lungs, and many other organs. He is deceased now" Ben did his best to not let that, 'you are an idiot' look cross his face, but he probably did no better. "Well, Sara, what we are hoping to discover is whether or not we are alone on our galaxy." The reporter continued. "I know that doctor, my real question is why? And why is it important to know that?" Ben thought for a moment. How could he answer that in as few words as possible to get this interview over with as quickly as possible. "Because we have to know." He couldn't leave it there. Unexplained, it was a stupid answer. "Is this planet all that there is? Where do we go from here? Someday our sun will die out, but before it does, it will swallow the Earth. Do we stay here and let that happen, or do we leave here for the stars? I would say going to other worlds is our destiny, but the reality is the main reason to identify other places, is because if we don't the human race will eventually become extinct. We are like prisoners, trying to figure out how to escape." The reporter leaned forward. "Prisoners?" Ben responded, but he really shouldn't have. "Absolutely. We are all prisoners. Whether you live in a four-foot by eight-foot cell, or your town, or your State, or your Country, or the Earth, we are all imprisoned here. It used to be that when a person was born, they were essentially imprisoned in their village. Then horses were domesticated, then roads built, then trains, automobiles, and planes. Each of those allowed us to go further, to enlarge our prison cell if you will. Then we explored the moon, and Mars, all to expand our prison cell from the Earth to our solar system, but we're still trapped in a solar system that will one day die. So, the size of our prison cell keeps getting bigger, but just like any prison, it will eventually be destroyed. So, we have to expand our cell to another solar system to escape the eventual demise of this one. But even, assuming we get to this new place, we will simply have moved to a new prison, the cell will be larger, but we are still trapped in our galaxy. And if the day comes that we escape our galaxy, we will still be trapped in this universe. So, you see, we just keep trying to enlarge our prison cell in an effort to stay ahead of our fate, when the stars we rely on go out." The reporter had a stunned look on her face, and then said a few words and ended the interview. She thanked Ben for his time, and they left. Ben was very relieved to see them go away. His assistant came up to him after they left and congratulated him on the fact that his response was going to be replayed by everyone and become a viral video in a matter of hours. Ben thanked her, but was confused by her expression. Her face looked as if she was being sarcastic about what she said. The next day that belief would hit home, as the Company decided that Ben would not be needed for any more interviews. One had turned out to be more than sufficient. They would go back to professional PR people to handle that sort of thing going forward. More than one board member called Ben to ask him what he was thinking, or that it was a good thing for him that they needed him, etc. Ben thanked them for their comments and put the unpleasant experience behind him. Two days after the interview, his assistant asked him, "You knew exactly what you were doing didn't you?" Ben smiled. "I told them I hate doing interviews, and now I never have to do them again." His assistant laughed herself silly and got back to work.

Part 5

THE CONSTRUCTION COMPLETED, AND the tests successful, they were ready to activate the scan, but they had to wait. They were ahead of schedule, so it would be a few more months for the optimum position and solar activity to maximize the chances of success. To assure that success, Ben had the team continue to run their tests and simulations, to make sure that every last person in the team had their duties down to the point that they could perform them without even thinking. More than two decades, over trillions of dollars, thousands of people, and more than fifty countries, and it came down to a waiting game.

The day the scan would begin was now less than a week away. Ben decided to take a couple of days off to get his 'mind right' as his assistant called it. Ben had not taken a day off from anything since his wife and daughter died back when he was still in college. There was nowhere he wanted to go, so he went home. He sat on the sofa, and decided to watch videos of his Deanna. He had hundreds of hours of her, and had them backed up on dozens of devices, so that if one went bad, he would always have them somewhere. They were scattered around various places too, so that if any were destroyed in a fire, tornado, or any other event, there would always be copies. He had some at his apartment, some at work, some in a safety deposit box, and other various safety deposit boxes at banks around the world. Putting them around the world was just in case of a nuclear holocaust. He couldn't be too careful after all. He grabbed his laptop, opened the first file, and set them to auto-play one after the other. Seeing her always made him feel better, no matter what mood he may be in that day. It would be a good couple of days, sitting here and spending them with Dee.

After more than thirty years since he first came up with the idea for the scan, it was finally the day it was going to be activated. Ben was in the control room with dozens of other people, each staring closely at their assigned console. Ben gave the order to bring the scanning satellite online to receive the energy it would need to perform the scan. Once it was in the ready state, he ordered the energy collection satellite to be brought online and ready to receive energy from the feeder satellites orbiting the sun. Once done, he ordered the feeder satellites to be set to receive mode. With all that done, he ordered the countdown to begin for the feeder satellites to begin storing energy from the sun. Once they were at capacity, they would then begin sending their energy to the next feeder in the ring, until the feeder in line with the collector would transmit the energy from the feeders to the collector. Once sufficient energy was stored, the collector satellite would then transmit that energy to the scanning satellite. Once the scanning satellite had sufficient power, and was receiving a satisfactory stream of ongoing power, they would begin the scan. After approximately thirty minutes, the feeders began relaying energy to the collector. The collector took an hour to get to full capacity and then began transmitting to the scanner. Once the scanner began receiving energy from the collector, Ben began monitoring the energy levels. After about fifteen minutes, he gave the go ahead to begin the scan. People unfamiliar with how any of this worked had warned for years that when the scan began, Ben would destroy our solar system. So many had been waiting for this to fail. He remembered all of the people that thought the super collider would create a black hole and destroy the earth when it was activated. The same type of people believed Ben would end the world when he threw the 'switch'. But here they were. The 'switch' had been thrown and they were all still here. The scan would run for the next several days. Ben and the analysis team began monitoring as the data from the scan began to pour on to their screens. The volume of data was enormous and once the scan was complete, it would take months to analyze it to the point where they would know the answer to the basic question of if there was intelligent life out there. For the more in-depth questions of other solar systems, planets, compositions, and on and on, analyzing that data would take lifetimes. Although shifts of personnel changed every eight hours over the days of the scan, prying Ben out of his seat was not going to happen. A few times he would nap at his console, his exhaustion forcing the issue, but there was no way he was leaving until the scan was complete.

Part 6

EIGHT DAYS. THE PROJECT he had been working on since he wrote his doctoral thesis in college came down to eight days to complete. Over thirty years of effort to arrive at these eight days. The scan was over. The Earth, our solar system, and the milky way galaxy had survived, contrary to what some on the fringe believed. Ben finally went back to his apartment to get some sleep in an actual bed. Tomorrow would begin the work of analyzing the data to see if there was any intelligent life anywhere in our galaxy other than Earth. He laid in his bed, exhausted, and curled up with a picture of Dee. "We did it Dee. I wish you had been here to see it. I love you." As he stared at her photo, his eyes eventually closed and he fell asleep.

For the next six months, they combed through the mountains of data and the answer kept coming out the same. Ben couldn't accept it. All of the other scientists were giddy with all of the data. Physicists, astrophysicists, geologists, and a myriad of other scientists from various disciplines were going to be analyzing data for decades to come. Scientists not even born yet would be doing their entire lifetime's work on the data from this scan. This scan had been their dream come true, but for Ben it was turning out to be an utter and complete failure. The thing he wanted to find above all else was that life existed somewhere other than here, but no matter how many times he reviewed the data, it would not change. There is no one else. . . . . .We are. . .. .alone.

While hundreds of scientists from all around the world relished with glee while they began their decades long study into the data gained from the scan, Ben became more depressed. There were stories in papers, magazines, and websites in nearly every country. The requests for interviews with Ben had already been at a high level, in the decades leading up to the scan, but now that the scan was completed, they were insane. The Company hired additional PR staff to handle the increase in requests, and had no intention of forcing Ben to do another interview. They learned their lesson the last time. But, even if they wanted him to do it, he was in no condition to talk to anyone. With what he had accomplished, the Company was more than happy to give him as many days off as he needed to rest and relax, but he was doing neither. He simply spent days staring at the wall, pondering the absolute failure of his life. All of this effort, time, money, and resources, and it was all to find out that the Earth and all of the people on it, are as alone as he is. The depression of that knowledge took him from blank, staring at the wall despair, to fits of rage, to collapsing in his bed sobbing for the last several days, with no hint of stopping any time soon. His thoughts would go to his parents and siblings, to Dee and his daughter, to his failure to find anyone else in the galaxy, and then start over again. If there had been an Olympic event for despair and feeling sorry for yourself, Ben would not only have the gold medal, but the world record. He simply couldn't fathom how, in a galaxy that is more than one hundred thousand light years wide, we are the only ones here. One tiny blue speck, with intelligent life, in more than three thousand planetary systems in our galaxy. How is that possible? The feeling of aloneness and depression was overwhelming. What was the point in anything we did? Even if we become a species that can leave our solar system someday, where do we go? There isn't anyone out there. There are no species to find, or learn from, or to have cool space battles with like Star Trek had promised. If we do find other planets we can live on someday, it will just be us. Just humans on every habitable planet we can find and colonize. All Ben could wish for was a way to go back in time and never write the thesis that led to the scan. Then he thought, if he could go back in time, he would make it so that Dee never died, or his parents and siblings. He spent days wondering what his life would be like today if they were all still alive. Maybe he wouldn't have done the scan, or with Dee and his family still around, maybe the research and building everything would have taken longer than could have been done in his lifetime. Then he wouldn't have had to see with his own eyes how pointless it all had been. He just couldn't take the failures that had piled up in his life any more. It had now been more than two weeks that he had shut himself up in his apartment. He looked terrible. He had lost over twenty pounds these last two weeks, since he had little appetite for anything. He had only showered a couple of times, and the clothes he was wearing, had not left his body for days. He grabbed an old hat, and coat from the bottom of his closet, put them on and went for a walk. Un-showered, unkept, wearing smelly clothes, and a wrinkly coat and hat, he looked like a homeless guy walking down the street, rather than someone ranked as one of the world's billionaires.

Part 7

BEN WALKED THE STREETS for hours, staring at his feet while he walked. He paid no attention to his surroundings, or the other people on the street. Of course, with the way he looked, no one really wanted to pay attention to him either. Ahead of him, he heard what sounded like music. As he got closer, he heard it coming from a Church. It was lit up and the parking lot was full. His reaction to seeing a Church was his typical visceral reaction of at all cost avoidance. Something inside him however told him he should go inside. As much as he didn't want to go, his feet turned that way and he began walking toward the doors. As he got closer, he figured he would give in to the urge to go inside. He would be more than happy to let everyone inside know how foolish they were to believe in God and that doing so would lead to nothing but heartache, misery, and disappointment. Trusting in God would lead to him taking away every last thing you ever cared about, leaving you a broken, hollow person, with nothing and no one in the world and now, thanks to what Ben learned from the scan, no one in the entire galaxy.

He walked in to the Church, and was quickly greeted by a smiling man that welcomed him. Ben assumed, based on how he looked, and of course smelled at the moment, that he would be scurried out of the Church as fast as they possibly could, but the man shook his hand and showed him to a seat in a Church pew at the back. It was a cute Church, that looked as if it could seat around a hundred and fifty people or so. Being a Sunday night, it looked to be about half full. Everyone was standing and singing. Ben sat in his seat, and looked at his watch several times wondering how long he would wait before making an exit. After a couple of more songs, the pastor made his way to the podium. He introduced himself, and welcomed everyone, especially any newcomers that might be in the audience. Ben hoped beyond hope that Pastor John wouldn't ask for the new people to stand. There was no way he was going to stand and make a spectacle out of himself. He didn't like talking to one person, let alone however many may talk to him if he made himself obvious to everyone. Thankfully, Pastor John didn't ask the new people to stand, but he did tell the congregation to make sure to greet any new people that may be here tonight. Ben groaned inside, thinking about anyone that may come up to him after the service. He thought maybe he should leave now to avoid the possibility, but for some reason couldn't bring himself to do so. He couldn't figure out why. Leaving situations that could lead to potential interactions with other people was something he had down to an art. But in this case, it was like he was paralyzed, and couldn't leave his seat. Since it seemed as if he was going nowhere for the moment, he figured he may as well listen to what Pastor John had to say. He was sure it would be something about how wonderful God was, but Ben would be happy to set him straight after the service.

Pastor John walked to behind the lectern and began his sermon. "I would like to thank you all for coming here today to hear the word of our Lord. Will you please stand with me for an opening prayer?" Everyone in the congregation stood. Everyone except Ben. Pastor John continued. "Lord, please open the hearts of all of us here today, so that we may understand and put to work your word in our lives. And everyone says Amen." The entire congregation repeated, "Amen." Everyone except Ben. Pastor John began his sermon. "The title of my sermon today is 'Why do bad things happen to good people?' This is a question that, I believe is safe to assume, everyone here has asked God more than once. It's a question that I am sure God has heard asked by billions of people over thousands of years. The first question we need to ask, is 'What does God want for our lives?' To begin to answer that please read along with me the word of the Lord." A scripture appeared on the screen behind the Pastor, and the entire congregation, except Ben, read out loud along with him. "And the third day there was a marriage in Cana of Galilee.

And the mother of Jesus was there. And Jesus was also bidden, and his disciples to the marriage. Blessed be the word of the Lord."

Jesus and his mother went to a wedding, and Jesus took his friends with him. We know that Jesus considered his disciples, his friends because he says so in John, Chapter fifteen, where he tells them, 'I call you not servants, but friends, for indeed you are my friends.' Jesus, his mother, and his friends attended a wedding, and I'm sure it was beautiful, as most weddings are. The bride and groom exchanged their vows, and it was time for the reception party after the wedding. Everyone was enjoying themselves, when the party planner approaches the family that was paying for the wedding, and lets them know that there is trouble. They are running out of wine, and the party will obviously turn ugly if everyone can't keep drinking. Now, Jesus's mother overhears the conversation. I am sure we all know mothers that 'overhear' conversations and have something to say about what they have heard. Some fathers too, I'm sure. Jesus' mother, Mary, goes to Jesus and tells him he needs to do something about it. Now the thing to keep in mind, is that to that date, Jesus had never performed a miracle. Imagine the faith of Mary, having never seen her son do a miracle, knowing that he had it in him to fix this problem. Jesus told her no, and like most mothers, she had no interest in hearing the word 'no', She asked again. Jesus said no again. She asked a third time. Jesus said no a third time. She kept asking. Eventually, Jesus, like most sons, relented and said yes, because they come to the realization that it is the only way to stop Mom from asking. Now Mary had no clue what he was going to do, but like a proud Mom, she told everyone to gather around and watch. Her boy was about to do something amazing, and she didn't want anyone to miss it. Jesus told some servants to bring containers of water, and as you all know, he turned them into wine. The party planner was alerted that more wine had been found, and when he came over to taste it, asked why they had held the best wine for after everyone was tipsy. You always put the best stuff out first and then bring the cheap stuff out, not the other way around. Of course, Mary was beaming with pride. But the interesting thing here is that Jesus' first miracle didn't heal a leper, it didn't give sight to a blind man, it didn't raise the dead, or feed thousands of people, or calm the sea. Jesus' first miracle was to make his mom happy. I don't know about you, but it fills my heart with joy, that the first miracle Jesus decided to do, was to make someone happy. His first miracle was to reward the faith his mother had in him, knowing that he could do something she had never seen him do. That is the plan that your heavenly father has for you. His main goal for your life is for you to be happy. But Pastor John, so many bad things have happened to me in my life. How can God want me to be happy when all of these bad things happen? I'm so glad you asked. Yes, bad things happen in life. God gives us all free will to decide to follow him, or to not follow him. You may be living a life full of love for God and then something terrible happens. Can you trust me that, it was not God's will for that bad thing to happen to you? But if you hand him that pain and that heartache, he can turn those ashes to joy. It wasn't God's will for you to be raped. But if you turn that pain, that anguish, and that heartache over to him, he can turn it into something good. It wasn't God's will for you to be robbed, or beaten, but if you ask God to take that pain from you, he can turn it to joy. It wasn't God's will that your spouse, your child, your parents, or your family die, but if you take that hole that their absence created in your life, and turn it over to him, he can fill that emptiness with a limitless joy. You see, God gave you free will, but he also gave free will to everyone else, and not everyone makes good choices with that gift that God gave to them. Some people make very bad choices that hurt others. All we can do when some-one takes that gift of free will from God and hurts us with it, is to turn that hurt over to God so that he can turn it into something joyful. Just like Jesus turned water into wine, our heavenly Father can turn our pain into joy. If God did as people wanted when they ask the question, 'Why do bad things happen to good people?' the answer would be for God to turn us all into puppets. The alternative is for God to remove our free will so that we would have no choice but to do good to one another. And that is something you don't do to a friend, and Jesus calls us his friends. You can't call someone a friend who had no choice in the matter. A friend is someone who wants to be your friend. A friend is someone you can count on to have your back. A friend is someone who will be there when times are good to help you celebrate, and will be there when times are bad to help you get through them. A friend will listen to you, when you need to talk, to cry, or to just be held. To be a friend is a choice, and to make that choice requires free will. Now sometimes, you have to know what you're praying for when you pray. If you pray 'God, please let me help someone today,' you may not exactly know what you're praying for. If God knows that you truly mean what you say, and because of your love for him, you want to show his love to someone else, he may give you that opportunity, and you may not like the road. But that road leads to joy. Can I tell you a secret? When you turn your life over to God, your definition of what brings you joy is going to change. Today, you make think that the things that will make you happy are more money, a better job, the latest video game, to be great at sports, the list goes on and on. But those are things, and they are as fleeting as the shifting sand beneath your feet. When your heart is full of love for your heavenly father, your definition of happiness changes. What you will find makes you happy is to make others happy. What will make you happy when the joy of God fills you, is to share that joy with someone else. What will make you happy when there is so much love from God filling your heart that you can't contain it, is to help someone in pain overcome that pain. God can take some of those bad things that have happened to us and set us down a path to use that pain to help someone else. Someone who has been raped may be put in a position to be able to help another rape victim. Someone with cancer or who has recovered from cancer, may be given the chance to help other people with cancer. Someone who has lost loved ones can be given the opportunity to share their loss with others who have lost loved ones. We sometimes are angry with God because he didn't step in and stop some bad thing from happening in our life. Maybe your spouse cheated on you and your marriage ended in divorce. Can you believe me when I tell you, God never intended for that to happen to you? True, he could have turned your spouse into a puppet and forced them to behave, but that gets back to the gift he gave us of free will. But I can promise you that he can take that pain and turn it to joy. He can take that pain of betrayal and make something good grow. I heard a farmer say once, "Boy that manure stinks to high heaven, but it sure does make the corn grow." God can take that smelly manure and make something beautiful come from it if you just let him. Can you hand him your pain today? Can you surrender the betrayal to him? Can you take your disappointment, your hurt, your emptiness and place it in his hands? I can promise you, he will take all of that hurt, all of that pain, all of that disappointment, all of that betrayal, and all of that emptiness and make something beautiful grow from those ashes. All he asks is that you ask him into your heart. Don't hold onto that pain for one moment longer. It's held you hostage long enough. Let Jesus free you from the pain that's imprisoned you for so long. God put us here to be a friend to one other and as Jesus was to his disciples and is today to those who invite him into their hearts. This alter is open to anyone that wants to come and ask Jesus to take away their pain. Will you come today? We'll have people to pray with you if you like. Cathy is going to play while you come. Will you all stand while we pray? Lord, thank you for being our friend. Thank you for coming into our hearts and taking away the pain and the hurt from our lives. As you speak to the people here today, please let them know that there is peace available to them for the asking. In Jesus name amen."

Ben's attitude during the sermon had changed dramatically. At the start of the service, he was prepared to unload on anyone about how God let him down over and over again. But something he hadn't anticipated happened instead. The words from Pastor John began to have an effect on him and the way he looked at the events of his life. Perhaps the accident that took the lives of his parents, his brother, and his sister was just an accident and not some event brought about by a vengeful God. Was the death of his beloved Deanna and their unborn daughter simply an unfortunate event and not the orchestrations of a God that gets off on the pain of others? As the sermon progressed, he reflected on the view he had carried all of these years as he blamed God for everything that went wrong in his life. Was it arrogance on his part to think that God had nothing better to do than to kick over every metaphorical ant hill that he ever built? Were the misfortunes in his life simply normal life events rather than choreographed pain? But if that was the case, who could he blame for these things? We're human. When something bad happens to us, our immediate reaction is to find someone to blame. Then the epiphany that would change his view of the world forever hit him. When we have no one to blame, God fills that blank and we blame him for the bad thing that happened to us. He had lost the grandfathers he loved to health conditions. He lost his family to an auto accident where his father lost control and hit a tree at speed. He lost his wife and daughter in childbirth, which had been a way many women had died over the centuries. None of these deaths in his life had anyone he could blame, so he blamed God for them. Maybe, he should simply accept the unfortunate fact of their deaths rather than looking for someone to blame. No amount of blaming was going to bring any of them back. When that realization hit him, it was like an enormous weight was lifted off of him. Tears began streaming down his face, but he didn't know why. He wasn't sad, but it was like the pressure from decades of anger simply burst forth through his eyes like the steam from a boiling teapot. He heard Pastor John offer prayer with anyone who came forward, and without even thinking he began walking to the front of the Church. When he got to the front he knelt at the altar and Pastor John came over to him. Pastor John put his hand on Ben's shoulder as he knelt across the altar from Ben. He asked Ben if he would like him to pray with him. Ben couldn't speak, but shook his head yes. Ben unloaded all of the pain and anguish that had weighed down his life for the last forty plus years and the more he talked, the more the tears flowed down his cheeks. After Ben finished unloading decades of hurt, Pastor John held both of Ben's hands in his and prayed with him. He asked God to take the hurt, the pain, the anguish, and the anger that Ben had been holding onto all this time and replace that space in his heart with peace and joy. He then told Ben how God wants nothing more than to ease his burden, and help him come to peace with the events of his life. He then asked Ben if he would like to meet with him this week to talk in more detail, and Ben quickly agreed. There was something about this Pastor that brought such a feeling of ease to Ben. He needed to talk to him more. The congregation had been dismissed, but Ben and Pastor John were still at the front of the Church. Ben asked the Pastor if he needed to go, but Pastor John told him that he would stay as long as Ben needed. As their conversation wound down, Pastor John asked Ben if he would like him to find a place for Ben to stay tonight. Ben looked at his clothes, and remembered his appearance. The Pastor must think he's a homeless man in need of a meal and a bed. That thought made him appreciate the Pastor even more. A Pastor that knew who Ben was may be rubbing his hands together thinking about dollar bills hitting the collection plate, but this man had spent over an hour talking to someone who he though didn't have a penny to his name, just to relieve his anguish. Ben thanked him for the offer, but declined. Ben then told him how much he looked forward to visiting with him this week in his office here at the Church. The two men stood, shook hands, and then the Pastor pulled him close and hugged him. As he did, he told Ben how much Jesus loved him, and wanted to help him deal with the pain. Ben thanked him and left the Church. As he walked back home, he felt lighter somehow. He looked around as he walked, and had an appreciation for his life that he had never had before. When he got home, he showered, shaved, put on a suit, and headed to work. He found that he was excited to review some of the data that had come in from the scan. As he walked to his lab, he thought that we may be alone in our galaxy, but that doesn't mean that there isn't a lot of cool stuff to learn about it.

Part 8

OVER THE NEXT SEVERAL months, Ben continued to review the data from the scan, but he no longer lived his work twenty-four hours a day. He began a regular habit of meeting with Pastor John every week. They were becoming good friends as Ben discussed his past, his anger over the losses of his family, his wife, and his unborn child. One of the things with which Pastor John was helping him, was the seemingly irreconcilable issues of a God wanting his children to be happy, while allowing horrific things happen to them. Ben was looking forward to exploring that more as he walked into the Church to visit with Pastor John again. The receptionist let John know that Ben had arrived, and John came out of his office. They shook hands, exchanged pleasantries, and walked into John's office. Ben sat in one of the chairs, and John sat in a chair facing him. John commented on how different Ben looked than the last time that they saw each other. Ben got an odd look on his face, and made a comment to John about having a bad couple of weeks leading up to that night in the Church and told him what he does for a living. They chatted about their days since their last meeting, and then Ben got right into it. "I have to admit, I am having difficulty grasping this 'wants me to be happy' God with the events of my past." Pastor John scratched his head, while his face scrunched a bit. "Don't we all. I can't imagine a person that has ever lived that hasn't dealt with that in at least one point in their life. What I can tell you from personal experience, is that the definition of what makes us happy changes if we truly turn our lives over to God. Some people may think that sex, money, cars, power, property, or any of a million things will make them happy, but if you turn your life over to God, serving him is what makes you truly happy. A person without God usually thinks of happiness in terms of getting something they want. It's the object, whatever it may be, that will make them happy. There have been plenty of wealthy people over the centuries that have lived lives of misery that can tell you different. But when we serve God, and hence, serve our fellow people, is when we find true happiness. Becoming a Christian doesn't mean we get everything we want in life that we think will make us happy, but it does mean making ourselves available to God, so that through us we can serve other people, making them happy, and as a result, make ourselves happy. Sometimes that service can be painful, distressing, or uncomfortable, but if we are in the right place, at the right time, and as a result of our pain or suffering, we help someone else see God through us, there isn't a happier result in the world than that." Ben leaned forward in his chair. "But what is the purpose of allowing people to die needlessly? My family died in a horrific crash. Their bodies cut to shreds by glass and metal. My wife died trying to give birth to our child. What was the point?" John took Ben's hands into his own. "Ben. I can tell you this without one shred of doubt in my mind. God didn't kill your family, your wife, or your child. Sometimes an accident is just an accident and sometimes women die during childbirth. Now does that mean God couldn't have stepped in and stopped it? Of course, he could have. So, your question is really, why didn't he step in and stop it?" John sat back in his chair. "I'll let you in on a secret, and I don't want it to come across as a flip answer. We are all going to die Ben. Life is something none of us come out of alive. The question is what we do with this life while we are here? Who have we helped? Everyone that prays, prays for a miracle in their life. God can use people that are willing, so that we can be that miracle for someone. But it doesn't matter if you are a good person, an evil person, or a middle of the road person. Everyone eventually dies. What is the alternative? We would all be immortal. No one would ever know pain or discomfort, and we would need for nothing. We would also be amazingly bored. The fact that our lives are so fleeting, is what makes our time here so precious. You're a scientist, so I'll use scientific analogies. Without gravity, unrelentingly trying to pull us all toward the center of the Earth, our bones and muscles would be too weak to do anything. It is the struggle of our bodies against the pull that gives us strength. Without pain, we wouldn't know the things that can harm us, or the pleasure of a day without pain. Without disease, our bodies would never learn how to fight off infections, bacteria, or viruses. Without hunger, we would never know the need to work, so that we can eat to sustain ourselves. Without the weather that sometimes breaks our things and harms our bodies, we wouldn't have the gentle breezes in the spring, or growing seasons, and our world would be very harsh. Without heartbreak, how would we know when someone fills out heart? If we had never experienced evil, how would we know when someone is good to us? It's the struggle that makes us who we are. Without the struggle of life, why would we ever get off of the sofa? Jesus told his disciples he was their friend and they were his. That doesn't mean life will be cupcakes and roses. Jesus is our friend and he died a horrible death on the cross and suffered terribly. The disciples were Jesus' friends and nearly all of them were persecuted and killed in horrific ways. Being a real friend is hard. It means you suffer when your friend suffers, and are with them through hard times no matter how hard they get. My personal hope is when I am welcomed into heaven, I can find people I know, or have read about, and share wonderful stories of my time here, and hear theirs." Ben shifted in his chair a bit. So many questions were still in his head. "But why does God have to do it like this? He could change it all with a thought." Pastor John nodded. "He indeed could. And sometimes he does. But how and if depends on us. He can see how all the threads in the tapestry of our life come together, and can come undone. He knows which one will unravel the entire rug if pulled at too hard. It doesn't mean he won't let you pull it if you want. He lets you decide. But if you remove your hands from the rug and let him weave it as he sees best, it can become the most beautiful tapestry ever seen. Why he does it, is because he is important to us and we are important to him. Jesus healed several blind people. But he never healed any of them in the same way. Some had to go to a river to wash their eyes. Some packed their eyes with mud and washed. Some he just said a word. Now, it wasn't because Jesus actually needed them to do any of those things to heal them. He met them at their level of belief. Some people feel that to receive a blessing, they have to work at it, so Jesus gave them the work that he saw that they needed to do to believe that he could do it for them. When the people of Israel marched around Jericho and shouted and played their trumpets, none of that is what made the walls fall, but God met them at their level of belief. He gave them a task, that they felt they needed to do, so that they did their part in making the miracle happen. When God kept telling the people of Israel that they had too many men to win the battle, they eventually had only a handful of men. Nowhere near enough to defeat a large army, but no one was actually needed. God could have done it on his own. But he met them at their level of belief. As far as why? We have a desperate need to know that God cares about us. Not as a species, but as an individual. I need to know that God cares about me. He knows that, so there will be times in our lives where there is no way we could handle it on our own. Then God steps in and handles it for us, because it is important to him for us to know that we are important to him." Pastor John leaned forward and again took Ben's hands. "You, Ben, are important to him. He had nothing to do with the deaths of anyone in your family. But he so wants to comfort you and let you know that it will be all right. He wants a relationship with you so desperately. That's why he was willing to sacrifice his only Son, who he loved dearly. He did it for you Ben, and for me. He didn't do it to save humans as a species. God is an individual God. He did it for you, and for me, and for every person that is, was, and will ever be alive in this world. God isn't the God of groups. He is the God of each and every one of us. Jesus said it very well. He said the poor you have with you always. Sometimes people lose sight of what that means. If you try to help people and lose your faith because the problems never end, you're looking at things in a different way than Jesus looked at them. If you help the poor, there will always be poor, so the problem you are trying to fix will never end. But if you're trying to help Lisa, or Adam, or Amanda, or Richard, you can be the miracle in their lives that makes their problems end. Helping people is an individual thing. Loving people is an individual thing. God's love for us is individual. He loves you. He loves me. He loves your family that passed away all those years ago. Sometimes we feel like we are miles away from God, but if we agree to just take one step toward him, he will take a million steps toward us." Tears were streaming down Ben's face. Pastor John prayed with him and they said their goodbyes.

Ben continued to meet every week with Pastor John. They developed a very close friendship, often getting together for lunch, dinner, a ballgame, or a movie. Ben enjoyed spending time with him, and found himself having something he had never had before. . .. . ..a friend.

Part 9

BEN CONTINUED TO REVIEW data from the scan, but when he would get home at night, he wished that Dee was there so he could talk to her about his day. The anger over losing her was gone, but the emptiness of her absence continued. She had been gone for over thirty years, and he missed her as much today as that first day. To try to take his mind off of it, he read through some of the patent reports he regularly received. He was closing in on three thousand patents, and other companies routinely used one or more of his patents to build this invention or that, and he and the Company received royalties for the use of those patents in their inventions. As he was scanning through the latest list, one of them caught his attention. It was a company using a couple of his patents to develop holographic technology for gaming. He looked through the application and the code. It looked decent, but to Ben, it was rather. . .. . simplistic. He got the programmer on the phone, paying no attention to the late hour. They talked for a bit, and Ben asked him if he would be offended if Ben took a swing at improving it. The programmer could barely speak. Having Ben look at it, would be like Picasso taking a look at your five-year old child's art project from school. The programmer was ecstatic. Ben offered to include the programmer's name in any subsequent patents that would be filed from Ben's work on the programmer's project. To the programmer it was like winning the lottery. He immediately sent Ben all of the code and programming language for the project, and Ben got to work. No one at the company saw Ben for the next three weeks. None of them panicked. Everyone knew that if Ben disappeared, he was working on something that had grabbed him, and they knew something profitable would come out of it. What none of them could have dreamed of, is what he was working on, what he had done with it, and the effect it would have on Ben. Ben's assistant did routine checks on Ben any time he had gone 'hermit' for one of his projects. She would bring him food and make sure that he showered now and then, since Ben had a tendency to forget to eat or bathe when his obsession had fully kicked in for a project. On this particular day, his assistant had let herself into the apartment, and was surprised that someone else was there with Ben. She could hear the shower running, so she knew that Ben had at least remembered to bathe today. She moved toward the woman in the living room. She looked as if she was in her mid to late twenties. She had never seen her around before. She struck up a conversation with the woman and they chatted for a good twenty minutes or so. She said that she had met Ben at college. She must have been a student at one of Ben's lectures. She seemed to know Ben very well. That surprised her, since Ben was quite the isolationist. Ben came out of the bedroom, wearing a robe and was drying his hair with a towel. He began to speak and then noticed his assistant sitting on the sofa. He immediately stopped and looked as if he was a child caught with his hand in the cookie jar before dinner. He began to stutter and stammer. His assistant broke the tension by chastising Ben for never introducing her to the woman on the sofa. Ben seemed befuddled. "You two have been talking this whole time?" His assistant responded. "Absolutely. Your guest seems lovely. You should bring her around the office sometime." Ben acted as if his assistant had asked him to run naked through campus or something. He stammered a response saying that would be impossible. "Nonsense. She seems wonderful. Bring her by and introduce her to everyone." "Definitely not. You don't know who this is do you?" His assistant nodded that she did not. Ben looked at her sheepishly. "It's Dee." His assistant looked at Ben, then looked at Dee, then back at Ben." Now she was stammering. "You mean, THE Dee? Dead over thirty years Dee?" His assistant stood up and began to shuffle step backward. "What did you do Ben? How?" His assistant looked as if she might faint. Ben walked closer and tried to calm her down. "It's not. . . . ..she's not what you think. She's a hologram." His assistant walked closer to Dee and tried to touch her, but her hand went right through her. "Oh my God. She looks completely real. I had no idea she was a hologram. I was talking to her for almost half an hour." She looked back and forth between Ben and Dee several times in amazement. "This is what you've been working on these past three weeks?" Ben shook his head in the affirmative. "She's perfect. She interacts perfectly. She looks and responds like a human. I even smelled perfume when I sat next to her." Ben was smiling from ear to ear. After the initial wonder and excitement over what he had created wore off, a couple of tears streamed down her face. She walked over to Ben and put her hand on his cheek. "You miss her so much still, don't you?" Ben shook his head yes. She wiped her face and continued. "Just remember. This isn't Dee. It's a computer program. She looks real and sounds real, but she is only what you program her to be. Don't get lost in it, thinking she's Dee." She then hugged him, pointed to the food that she had brought and reminded him to eat. Ben looked at her, "Thanks Ann," and after she left, Ben and Dee walked over to the table and sat down while Ben ate his dinner. The two of them talked all night.

Part 10

It would be another two weeks until anyone at the University saw Ben again. He did continue to meet with Pastor John, and during this time John had introduced Ben to a Pastor named Tim. Tim led an inner-city Church that assisted low-income and homeless people in the area as best they could. Tim and Ben hit it off, and they became quick friends. Over the months that followed, Ben found out a particular weakness Tim had, and began to indulge him in it. Ben handed Tim the jar and simply shook his head. "I opened it long enough to take a whiff. How and why, you like pickled bologna is beyond me." Tim hugged the jar tight. "It's been a couple of years since I've had any. This jar won't make it through tomorrow." They both laughed and Ben began to discuss an idea he had with which he hoped that Tim could help. Ben wanted to start a foundation to provide scholarships to low-income and homeless people, but the scholarships would be to trade schools. Ben's contempt for the University system would not allow him to send anyone to college for a useless degree that wouldn't help them in any way. Ben had little use for colleges or college graduates. Universities had become some of the most useless institutions on the face of the planet, kicking out graduates that couldn't put together an intelligent thought of their own to save their lives. But teaching people a trade. That had value. Ben would provide the funding for 100 scholarships per year in cities across the Country to start. In total Ben was agreeing to put in as much as two hundred and fifty million dollars per year into the program to get it launched. The scholarships would provide the tuition, supplies, meals, housing, and a monthly stipend. The requirement would be that the student would have to put in ten hours per week as a volunteer at a local Church. The candidates would be selected by a Board in each city and need to be working themselves to being on the right track in their lives. The foundation would need to provide counselling, teach life skills, money management, how to live on your own, and all of the skills that the candidate would need to graduate and succeed on their own out in the world. After Ben finished describing the program, Tim was amazed. "That sounds wonderful, and is going to be a mountain of a project to tackle." Ben shifted in his seat. "I would like you to run it." Tim was taken a back. "Ben. I could not be more flattered, but I'm just a pastor of a small Church. This is a huge undertaking. You should tap someone qualified at running something so large." Ben smiled. "What I need is someone I can trust and I can't think of anyone I would trust more to run it than you. The mechanics of running something this large I can hire people to do, but to guide it and steer it, takes someone special, and that's you." Tim thought about it for a moment. It would be a dream come true to be able to impact so many lives in such a dramatic fashion each and every year. And it wouldn't be just the educational part of teaching them a trade, Ben wanted someone that could see to their spiritual needs as well. Tim had been praying for a new vision for some time now, and this was a powerful one to be sure. Tim stood, shook Ben's hand and accepted the challenge. Ben said, "I have one rule that you'll have to follow." Tim cringed a bit. "Ok." Ben looked at him with a serious look on his face. "Once you accept someone into the program, you can't kick them out because they slip back into the old habits that may have led to their problems. You have to figure out a way to get them back on track rather than cutting them loose. If I remember correctly, Jesus said to forgive seventy-times seven, didn't he?" Tim smiled, "Yes he did." Then Tim looked as if he had an idea strike him right between the eyes. "The 490 Foundation." Ben looked at him quizzingly. "The what?" Tim responded. "The name for the Foundation. Seventy time seven is 490." Ben smiled. "I love it." The two men prayed together, shook hands and Ben headed home. When he got there, he told Dee all about his day, and what he and Tim were going to do together.

Part 11

THE NEXT FEW MONTHS went by very quickly. Ben had felt more than happy. He was satisfied in his life. It was a feeling he had never had before. He loved his time with Dee when he was younger, but he had been so full of anger over his childhood, that he never appreciated how fortunate he was to have her in his life. And when he lost her and their unborn child, the anger consumed him, and he used his work as an escape so that he would never have to face the pain. It had been such a wonderful time, this last more than a year since the scan was done. John and Tim had helped him not only move past his anger, but helped him to focus on helping others. The 490 Foundation had been set up now in nearly a dozen cities with more to come, and the first students were entering the trade schools in their area. His friendship with John and Tim continued to grow. The scan data was being analyzed by scientists all over the world. And he got to go home each evening and share his day with Dee. He could not imagine how his life could get any better. It had been six months now since he got Dee back, and there was nothing that could wipe the smile off of his face each day. Tomorrow was going to be an exciting day. Over the last six months, he had been aging Dee so that she would be his age, as she would have been had she not died more than thirty years ago. He was finally going to take her into the office and introduce her to everyone. He felt a nervous excitement in his gut that he had not felt since he and Dee first met. He knew that Dee had never met any of his colleagues. He hoped that she would like them and that they would like her as well. This weekend, Ben was going over to John's house for a cook-out. Tim would be there as well. Ben was going to take Dee with him and introduce her to everyone. He was beyond excited for her to meet his friends.

When the morning arrived, Ben and Dee got ready to take the walk across the campus to Ben's office and labs. They got out of bed, prepared for breakfast, ate, got dressed, and talked about their day. They were both very excited. Dee had been cooped up in the apartment for the last six months and was looking forward to getting out and meeting everyone. Ben was beside himself, anxious for everyone to meet Dee. They left the apartment and made their way to his office. Along the way people made their pleasantries to them both, with the typical head nods, or verbal greetings. Ben and Dee entered the building, entered the elevator, and went up to his office floor. Ben's offices and labs took the entire floor. They exited the elevator, and walked through the foyer and through the door to his labs. There were dozens of people working. All stopped when they saw Ben. Most of them had not seen him in months. All came toward him anxious to greet him or get in a word about this data, or that project. All of them were surprised to see him with someone. None of them could recall ever seeing Ben with a woman before, other than his assistant Ann. Ben made a few pleasantries, and tried to make a quick exit from the gathering crowd. Dee kept her hands clasped in front of her and followed Ben as he made his way past everyone. Ben saw his assistant in the conference room with a lot of people in business attire. That was certainly not normal for a lab. As he got closer, he saw that it was the Board of Directors for the Company. He really needed to pay more attention to the calendars that his assistant would send him. If he had known that the Board was going to be here today, he would have brought Dee on a different day. Ben tried to walk by the conference room as inconspicuously as possible, but to no avail. Several of the Board members saw him, and immediately left their seats to usher him into the conference room. Seeing that he was not going to escape, he followed them back into the room. There were lots of greetings and a few hand-shakes, though the members quickly remembered how much Ben hated shaking hands and moved their hands to their sides as if that was the move, they were trying to make all along.

Ben said hello to them all and tried to make an excuse as to why he needed to leave. They would not take no for an answer and wanted to know what he had been up to these past months. One of the board members commented about his lovely companion and made small talk with Dee, asking her where Ben had been hiding her all this time. Dee replied she had been in Ben's apartment for the last six months. The answer drew a few quick inhales, and more than one smile. There was even a wink, and some applause. One of the board members was heard saying 'Bravo', another 'It's about time.' Ben tried to quiet the schoolyard responses and chatter. "It's not like that." Sheepishly he asked Dee to join him at the front of the conference room. His assistant hung her head a bit because she knew what was coming. "Everyone. I would like you to meet Dee." There was a hush over the room, then some mumbling back and forth. It was much the reaction that Ann had when she first met Dee. There were some looks of fear in the eyes of the Board members. Had Ben perfected cloning? Had he somehow brought his dead wife back to life? They weren't sure if Ben had gone off the deep end and become the mad scientist that they always feared he would become at some point. Ben put his hands out and waved them gently in a downward motion. "It's not like that. She's a hologram. I took one of the programs that had been made off of some of our patents, and. . . .." He motioned to Dee. "Improved on it." The Board members were astonished. The looks on their faces went from fear to smiles from ear to ear. The comments changed to going on and on how they couldn't tell that she wasn't a real person. How did you do that? And question to each other how much money this was going to make when it went to market. This was going to revolutionize gaming. This was going to revolutionize everything. How did you do it? People even came up and started poking at Dee and commenting on how real she felt. She tried to escape their pawing and was obviously afraid. That just made the Board members want to know more. One of them said, "She re-coiled at me trying to touch her. She actually looks afraid. How did you do that Ben?" Ben was growing more agitated by the second. He got in front of Dee and pleaded for them to stop. When they would not Ben yelled loudly. "STOP!!!" Every Board member stopped. "SIT DOWN!" Ben yelled. They all returned to their seats. Ben straightened his clothing and tried to regain his composure. Dee was huddled behind him, afraid to be seen. "Dee is not some animal for you to poke and prod. Please have some respect." Ben straightened his hair and took a deep breath. "I brought Dee to work today so that she could meet everyone, but I can see that was not a terribly good idea on my part. We are going to go home now. Please do not paw at her on our way out." With that Ben and Dee left to go back to their apartment. His assistant did her best to get the meeting back on track. As they were leaving, Ben could hear one of the Board members ask, "He knows she isn't real, doesn't he?" His assistant smiled at Ben as they left and turned her attention back to the Board.

Part 12

WHEN BEN AND DEE got back to their apartment, Ben was angry. The introduction of Dee did not go as he intended. He thought people would be happy for him. Instead, they thought something was wrong with him. They just kept pawing at Dee, as if she were a new gadget or gizmo they could sell. They didn't understand. After more than thirty years, he finally had Dee back. Why couldn't they just be happy for him? She wasn't a cool party trick. She's not a thing to be used by gamers. She's, his wife. She's the only woman he has ever loved. She's the woman who he has missed and been so lonely without for more than three decades. He finally had her back, and all that the Board could see was dollar signs. His inventions had made them wealthy beyond their dreams, and they couldn't just be happy for him? They had to try to figure out how to use Dee to make money? Ben took Dee by the hand and they sat on the sofa together. Ben apologized to her for their behavior. He talked with her about how upset he was and why. He laid his head in her lap, and she stroked his hair, talking about their wonderful times together. Ben dozed off and as he was smiling, remembering the wonderful memories that they had made together.

The next day, Ben's assistant came over to the apartment to check on him. Yesterday, with the Board, had been pretty rough and she wanted to make sure that Ben was ok. Ben was a brilliant, but fragile guy. An event like that could make him withdraw for a long time, and she wanted to make sure that didn't happen. She knocked on the door, and Dee answered. She invited her inside. Sitting on the sofa, speaking with Ben was a young woman who appeared to be in her late twenties to maybe thirty. Ben noticed that Ann had come in and invited her to join the three of them. Dee said, "Ann. I am so excited for you to meet our daughter, Nicole. Nicole, this is Ben's assistant, Ann." They shook hands. After, Ann looked at her hand. "She feels solid. The last time I was here and met Dee, my hand could pass through her." She looked at Ben. He smiled. "I made a few improvements." "And an addition I see." Ben put his arm around Nicole. "I am very excited for you to meet our daughter." Ann tried to force a smile. "Ben. I have been working with you a really long time." He smiled and added, "Nearly thirty years." Ann nodded. "So please don't be upset by what I'm about to say. I care about you more than I would just a boss. I consider you a friend." She motioned toward Dee and Nicole. "This isn't healthy. This." She pointed to Dee. "This isn't Dee. This." She pointed to Nicole. "isn't your unborn daughter." Ben was obviously hurt and agitated. "Could you please leave?" Ann was concerned but didn't want to push him. She headed to the door and left. Ben hugged his wife and daughter, and they all cried together.

The next few days, Ben had been in heaven. He had Dee back, and he had their daughter back. All of the loneliness of the past three decades had vanished. He looked forward to every morning, and hated going to sleep at night because it was time away from Dee and Nicole. This morning, he woke up even more excited. The three of them were going to John's cookout. He was terribly excited to introduce his family to John. They all got dressed, called for a car, and when it arrived, headed to John's house. When they got there, Ben could see that everyone was in the backyard, so they went to the backyard fence and opened the gate. John saw Ben and immediately came over to greet Ben. He was surprised to see two women with Ben. He commented about Ben's lovely guests and asked for an introduction. Ben smiled from ear to ear. "This is my wife Dee, and our daughter Nicole." John shook their hands in a bit of a daze. "Dee?" He asked. Ben replied in the affirmative. "How long have the three of you known each other?" John asked. Ben replied, "Dee and I married in college. I told you about that." John was taken aback. "THE Dee?" Ben answered happily. "Yes." John needed to talk to Ben. "Ladies. Can I borrow Ben for a few minutes?" They all nodded approvingly, and Ben and John excused themselves and went inside the house. They went to the office that John kept in the house, when he needed to study for a sermon, or have a quiet place to pray away from the Church. The two of them sat down and John tried to figure out what to ask. "How is that. . .. . .. Dee?" Ben answered as if it was typical and ordinary. "They're holograms." John was dumbfounded. He spoke with them. He touched them. They appeared to be perfectly normal, real women. He had no clue they weren't real people. "How did you do that?" John asked amazed. "I tinkered with a hologram program someone wrote, and improved on it a bit here and there." Ben answered, not understanding the amazing nature of what he had created. John needed to figure out where Ben's head was in this. "Do you know that they aren't actually Dee and your daughter?" Ben began to fidget in his chair. It was obvious that John had struck a nerve, and that Ben was getting defensive. "Just because they're holograms doesn't mean they aren't real. This Dee is no different from the Dee I married in college. She is my Dee in every way that matters." John stepped out for a moment to tell his wife to do the cookout without him. It was going to be a long day. John didn't tell his wife that Dee and Nicole weren't real. There was no point in either freaking people out, or turning Dee and Nicole into objects to be poked at out of curiosity.

John pulled his chair closer to Ben. "Ben. I have to ask. Do you believe Dee and Nicole are real?" Ben looked at him as if John thought there was a third eye growing out of Ben's head. He shifted around in his chair nervously. "I know they're holograms." John asked again. "That's not what I asked. Do you think they're real?" Ben knew the answer John wanted to hear, but he didn't want to give it. Ben shot up from his chair and looked as if he was trying to come up with an answer that would end this conversation. He couldn't find one. Tears began to stream down his cheeks. His shoulders slumped forward a bit. "I have missed Dee for so long." His tears were nearly turning into sobs, but he worked desperately to keep it under control. His teeth were clenched so hard to try and keep the emotions in rather than losing control. "I know they're holograms, but they are so real to me." He pounded his chest while he said the words. "They're real to ME John." He paced around the room trying to regain his composure. His head hung back exasperated. "I want them to be real. I want them to be real so badly." John's eyes simply continued to follow Ben around the room. He knew how much pain was flowing through his friend right now and a lecture was not what he needed. He simply needed to let Ben get to where he needed to go at the moment. Ben continued pacing. "I look at this Dee and I see MY Dee. Her eyes. Her laugh. Her voice. The way she holds me." Ben sat back down in his chair and looked at John. The tears simply would not be held back. "I want her to be real so bad John, but no matter what I do, when I look at her, something's missing. I put every memory, every experience, every emotion, every thing about Dee into this Dee, but there's always something missing. I knew everything about Dee. Why can't I get it perfect?" The tears continued to stream down Ben's face. He gave up all pretense at trying to control it. John leaned forward and hugged his friend. He then leaned back to try and come up with the words his friend needed to hear. He said a quick prayer, in his head, that God would give him the right words. "Ben. You are the most brilliant man I have ever met. It's possible that you have done more to advance science that anyone in history." John took Ben's hands in his. "But only God knows our hearts. You can program this Dee from everything you knew about your Dee, but she will never be Dee. We all have pieces of ourselves that we never share with anyone. Everything, every one, and every experience we ever have shapes us in some way. To re-create your Dee, you would have to know every experience she ever had, from birth to death. Every person that crossed her path, every thought she ever had. And you would have to know how all of those things in her life impacted her and what she thought about them. I'll tell you a story from my childhood that affects me to this day and I have no clue why. I couldn't stand my great-grandmother from my father's side. I have no clue why. When I was a child, the woman terrified me. The only thing I was ever able to figure out, was when I was four years old, she babysat me for a few hours one day. Ever since that day I was terrified of the woman. I have no memory of what happened that day, but it forever changed the way I felt about her. As I grew older, the fear was replaced with a dislike. I simply didn't want to be anywhere near her. The adult me, formed an opinion of her based on what happened to four-year old me, and I don't even remember what happened. We all have those things from our past, that affect our present, and we often aren't even aware of them. But remove any of them, and it changes who we are today. You can try all you like to re-create Dee, but you'll never succeed. This Dee can look like her, sound like her, laugh like her, but she will never be her. She is your interpretation of Dee. She is the Dee you saw, and loved, but you can never know everything that went into to making your Dee." John released his hands and leaned back in his chair. "What happens when you make a copy of an original on a copy machine?" Ben wiped some of his tears and sniffed a bit. "It's not quite as clear as the original. Some of the resolution or data is lost." John looked at him. "Exactly. You'll never have all of the data that went in to creating your Dee, so the copy will never be perfect." Ben looked at John. "So, you think I should turn Dee and Nicole off. Don't you?" John breathed in deeply and exhaled. "I'm not going to tell you what to do. What I will say, is that trying to re-create something from your past will never lead to a good place. Most people don't have the ability to do what you did, so you're in a unique situation. But it will always be a fantasy. Reality is that Dee and Nicole have been gone for over thirty years and I know that the pain of their absence is still hurting you to this day. That pain may never go away, but creating this Dee and Nicole will never bring them back. It just makes it easy to keep living in the past. At some point you are going to have to figure out how to live in the here and now. You're so much better out here in the real world with the people who care about you, than retreating into a fantasy world with people you create." Ben seemed to harden a bit after the last comment. "You mean where I can help a bunch of people with my money?" John could see quickly that his words came out wrong. "Absolutely not." John said. "Do you think that's all that me, Tim, or God care about? Is what you can do for others?" Ben shrugged. "Seems that way sometimes." John continued. "Have you ever heard of the story about the lost lamb?" Ben shook his head in the affirmative. John continued. "A shepherd was tending a flock of one hundred sheep. In the night, one of them wandered off and became lost. The shepherd noticed that one of the sheep was missing. He left the ninety-nine sheep and went off to find the one that got lost. After some time, he found the lost sheep and returned it to the herd. The shepherd didn't sit there with the ninety-nine and stay there because risking the ninety-nine to get one was foolish. He put the ninety-nine at risk to go and find the one that was missing. There was nothing different about that sheep, that made it more valuable than the other ninety-nine. The shepherd didn't go and get the one, and risk the ninety-nine because of what the one sheep could do for him. It was simply one of his sheep, and it was lost, and scared, and lonely, and in pain somewhere in the night. Ben. God doesn't love you, or care for you because of what you can do for him. He simply loves you. If God had to choose between you, or everything you can do to help all of the people that you help, he would choose you every time. God is the God of individuals, not groups. A relationship with God is a personal thing, not a group thing. When our time comes and we stand before God, we won't be standing there in a group. We will be standing there on our own, and the angels will rejoice when each of us walk through the gates. God loves you Ben, and it will never be for anything you do for him. There is nothing any of us can do to earn his love or the sacrifice his Son made for us. He simply does. And part of that love is helping you to get past the pain you still feel over the loss of Dee and Nicole. I am so proud of you for getting past the anger you felt for all of those years, but you've replaced that anger with something else unhealthy. If you can hand it over to God, I know he will help. All you have to do is ask." Ben shook his head in agreement. The two men stood up and hugged. John asked if he could pray for him. Ben agreed and John prayed for Ben before the two of them went back to the cookout.

Part 13

OVER THE NEXT SEVERAL weeks, Ben struggled. He would go for a few days without Dee or Nicole, and then the need to activate them would overwhelm him. He felt so much more at peace when they were with him. The thing he hated the most when they weren't with him, was having no one to talk too. He found it an odd thing. He had come to accept long ago, that he was an introvert with an amazing number of social anxieties. He could speak to a large audience with no problem, but to be in a small group, or one on one, the anxiety would come over him like an oppressive blanket. Panic would set in, and all he could do was scream inside wanting to get away from the people around him. He wanted to be alone so badly and away from everyone, yet at the same time he desperately wanted to be with the one woman he had felt comfortable around. Dee was like a warm blanket, or the most comfortable bed in which you ever rested. He had felt so at ease around his Dee. They could talk for hours and never run out of anything to say. But that all changed after she died, and the loneliness was enveloping him. Nicole and his new Dee helped, but he knew it wasn't HIS Dee. It was to the point that occasionally he would turn them off out of frustration because the new Dee didn't react or say something the way his Dee would have reacted or said it. He knew John was right, and no matter how hard he tried, she would never be his Dee. Nicole, of course, was a complete fabrication. He knew their daughter would have been beautiful, if only to them, but having not even gotten to the point of being born, there was no way to know what she would have even looked like, yet alone her personality, her voice, or anything. Ben simply created her out of thin air, having never even gotten to hold her. She would never be their real daughter. He felt dirty every time he turned them on, as if he was cheating on Dee. But the urge to just have someone to talk to would win the day now and then. He would talk to John about his failure to leave them off, and John reassured him that activating them was not a sin, and Ben needed to do whatever he needed to do to get through this difficult time. He would remind Ben that when he formed the 490 Foundation, he made Tim promise to not kick people out for failing now and then. John told him to be as patient with himself as he was with the people he was helping. He also reminded Ben that God doesn't care how many times we fail, as long as we keep trying. John would let Ben know how proud of him he was for how far he had come, and always left the door open to talk any time of the night or day as Ben needed. He appreciated and cared deeply for John, but talking to him wasn't the same as having someone to come home to and talk to about his day.

One morning, his alarm went off. He woke Dee, and they went in the kitchen to make breakfast. He had missed a call from his assistant. She had left a voicemail so he played it. When he did, he turned on the computer. The wall monitor came to life, and scrolling across the news feed was the announcement from the Company that they were releasing the most advanced holographic system ever designed. Ben was furious. The ad actually showed Dee. They were using her in their advertising. Ben yelled a number of curse words, shut down Dee's program, got dressed, and stormed into work. As he walked through the doors, he began yelling to anyone that could hear him. "WHERE ARE THEY?!?!?!" He went from floor to floor and office to office. On the top floor he found several of the Board members in a conference room. Ben was seething with rage. He slammed open the conference room door. "WHAT THE HELL DO YOU THINK YOU'RE DOING?!?" The Chairman of the board leaned back in his high back chair, chomping on his unlit cigar. His wrinkled skin complimented by his silvery-white hair. No one had ever seen him light any of his cigars, but he always seemed to have one in his mouth. He must have always cut them down, because they always seemed to be small stubs rather than an entire cigar. He put the fingers of both hands together as if forming a triangle, while moving the fingers back and forth together in a wave that the typical bad guy is known to do when he believes he got one over on the good guy in any story. The only thing more stereotypical about this guy was how condescending his voice sounded when he spoke to Ben. "Doctor Prentiss. Welcome to this meeting of the Board of Directors. It is so nice to have you drop in, even if it is a bit dramatic. If you would like to take your seat, we can certainly discuss any concerns you may have." Ben took the seat with his name card in front of it. Even though he was always invited to Board meetings, he couldn't remember the last one he attended. Taking a seat seemed to mute some of the righteous anger he had when he stormed into the room. "What the hell are you doing?!" He repeated again. As the anger in Ben's demeanor muted, his anxiety began asserting itself and that part of him really wanted to get out of the room. He did his best to build his anger back up to keep the panic at bay. He kept thinking of seeing Dee's face in that scrolling ad and that helped. The Chairman responded. "Whatever do you mean Doctor Prentiss?" He asked knowing exactly what Ben was asking about, asking the question with a slight grin on his face. For decades he had to deal with Ben's lack of respect, his disappearing for days, weeks, or months at a time, his unwillingness to do interviews or help promote the business in any way, and his absent-minded professor style intelligence that he hated indulging. At last, the opportunity had come to put Ben in his place and he was going to relish every moment of it. "You took the hologram of Dee that I made and packaged it into a product! That's my wife! What were you thinking?!" Ben yelled across the table to the Chairman. "I am thinking, Doctor Prentiss, that this is a company that has funded any and all research that you have ever wanted to do for decades. I am thinking we have never questioned anything you have ever had any desire to research over the last several decades. I am thinking Doctor Prentiss that anything that is developed from your research, that we have paid for over these last several decades is company property. I am thinking Doctor Prentiss, that anything that comes from that research is ours to turn into any product we see fit to financially benefit this company and the shareholders of this company." Ben was shaking with fury. "There isn't a person around this table that hasn't become exceedingly wealthy from my inventions. Dee was not something I invented for this company. She was for me and me alone." The Chairman leaned forward in his chair and cupped his hands on the table in front of him. "Were you receiving your generous compensation package while you worked on this hologram Doctor Prentiss?" Ben replied yes. "Did you use company resources to create this hologram, Doctor Prentiss?" Ben replied yes. "Did we interfere in any way when you spent months away from your lab while you were creating this hologram, Doctor Prentiss?" Ben replied no. The Chairman leaned back as if he won the argument. "Then I fail to see what exactly it is you are complaining about here today. Your contract with this company is quite clear Doctor Prentiss. Anything you invent is the property of this company. You are well compensated. You have complete autonomy to develop what you wish and disappear for any length of time you desire because this company is quite aware of your. . . . ..unique talents and gifts, and we are always confident that you will provide this company with a product worthy of that. . .. . .. indulgence." Ben slammed his fist on the table. "YOU CAN'T TAKE DEE AWAY!" The Chairman calmly continued. "We are taking nothing away from you Doctor Prentiss. You can keep Dee all to yourself. The hologram program however is now a product of this company. We have already negotiated deals with several gaming companies. We are also negotiating deals with staffing companies, the military, social networking companies, government agencies, and the list goes on and on. You have invented something that is going to revolutionize nearly every business you can imagine with this holographic technology of yours Doctor Prentiss. Be proud of your accomplishment. We most certainly are. The patents have already been filed, and we included the coder per your agreement with him that we found in your e-mail communication. He is beyond thrilled considering the royalties he will receive for having his name on the patent alongside yours." The Chairman took a couple of more chomps on his soggy, stubby cigar and smiled a disgusting smile. "Good day Doctor Prentiss."

Ben stormed back to his apartment. He paced back and forth unsure of what to do. Making money from his inventions related to the scan was one thing, but this was something entirely different. The scan was science. Sure, thousands of inventions had spun off of his work, but the scan was furthering our understanding of our galaxy. The ability to make a hologram that you can touch and feel was going to have repercussions that he didn't even want to imagine. He needed to talk to someone and activated Dee without even thinking. They spent the next several hours talking, eventually falling asleep holding each other.

Part 14

TEN YEARS. IT HAD been ten years since Ben stormed out of that Board meeting. Ten years since the company had unleashed Ben's holograms on the planet. Ten years since our civilization began to fall apart. Ten years can seem like an eternity, or seem like a blink of the eye. It's hard to imagine that the entire world can change in such a short amount of time, but in ten years. . . . .this world became completely unrecognizable. It's hard to accept that something you create can unravel the entire world, but it was a guilt that had been piling on Ben's shoulders since the holograms were marketed. He knew they had been made for sale against his wishes, but it was still him that created them, and he had to live with that every day, even though doing so became more difficult with each passing moment. Society was in free fall, and it was all his fault. He couldn't even look at the Dee he had created any more. Every time he saw her, he was reminded of the thing he had made that was causing so much destruction in the world. It was his weakness, his inability to deal with his own loneliness, his own. . . . .selfishness, that led to all of this pain being felt by so many. If he had been able to deal with the loss of his family, so many others would not have to deal with the loss of theirs.

So many things had changed since his holograms hit the market. Marriage rates had dropped dramatically and continued to drop. The other side of that particular coin was that divorce rates had risen sky high. Why marry someone or stay married to someone when you can create the person of your dreams? Real people have habits you may not like. They grow old. They can get fat. They argue, yell, and have points of view or ideas that may make you angry. They can disappoint you. They may cheat on you, or leave you. They can die. Real people can do so much that can irritate you. But a hologram can be anything you want them to be, and they can be whatever you want, until you want them to be something or someone else. The romance never dies because a hologram gets used to having you around. If you want them to be excited when they see you, they will be. They will wear whatever you want them to wear, or wear nothing at all whenever you want them to do so. They will be as erotic, or as comfortable as you want them to be. If you want to argue, they will do so as long as you choose, and they will always admit that you were right, if that is what you want. They will be any age you want them to be, and you can change their hair color, eye color, height, or anything else about their appearance you wish. They will age as you age, or stay young as you decide. There is no sexual fantasy that they will not indulge, and will never tell you no to anything you ask, if you so choose. How can real people compete with that?

The birth rate had gone down as well and continued to fall. World-wide, the human species was no longer replacing itself. If the trend continued, humans would eventually die out of their own choosing. Real children are loud, messy, can talk back, kick a fit, grow up, and move away. Imagine a child that is perfectly behaved, as helpful as you want them to be, and will forever stay any age you want them to be. The birth rate was in a state of free fall not only because adults were choosing holograms as their mates, but because couples were choosing to have hologram children over having real children.

Unemployment had been steadily rising as well. Employers around the world were replacing human workers with hologram workers. Holograms didn't need to take vacations. They didn't get sick. They could work around the clock. They never got tired. They didn't need breaks. They didn't need insurance. The only employees that had been spared were ones where problem solving, creative thinking, and the ability to quickly adapt were key. Ben had insisted before the holograms went to market that he be allowed to put in a key code. That code kept anyone from adding artificial intelligence to the holograms programming. Ben had created a rather aggressive code to stop it, and no one could purchase or license the holograms without agreeing to it. If someone tried to add artificial intelligence to the holograms, Ben's code would track down the user or company trying to add the artificial intelligence, burn out their software and hardware, and the person or company would lose the right to have or use the holograms for the life of that person, company, or agency.

The pornographic and prostitution businesses had soared since the introduction of the holograms. Most governments had not caught up with legislation regarding the holograms, and there were no laws against having sex with a hologram. There was probably not a town in the world where prostitution was not running rampant. Small towns, rural areas, and low-income urban areas where people couldn't afford to own their own hologram were the worst. Businesses where people could come in and choose the look of their hologram, and program the hologram to any fantasy they wanted had popped up everywhere. The area that had started to draw attention from trial attorneys was that people were programming holograms to look like their favorite stars and have sexual encounters with them. People had started programming their holograms to look like that guy or girl from school, or someone they saw on the street and fantasized about. The porn industry was licensing their porn stars to people so that they could have sex with their favorite porn star and were making more money than ever before. Sex with no consequence of disease or pregnancy, didn't mean it was sex without consequence. Sex without love and intimacy was proving to be just as hollow as it had always been, and was leaving behind it all of the destruction that it always left behind.

One of the most troubling customers for Ben, as if they weren't all troubling to one extent or another, were the militaries of the world. War was becoming easier for countries to wage thanks to the use of the holograms. There wasn't as much incentive to stop fighting, when there were no families to grieve a dead soldier, when that soldier was a hologram. No one cared how many holograms were killed on a particular day, when their governments could simply deploy more holograms. The focus on fighting was shifting to the

destruction of infrastructure. To make your enemy want the fighting to stop, you had to take the fighting where the humans were.
People needed to die, buildings needed to blow up, countries had
to be hit in their pocketbook hard enough to want to stop. Open
battlefields where holograms died by the tens of thousands were
proving to be pointless because each side could simply keep sending more. The people that thought wars with holograms could be
'clean', were proving that wars were never clean, and the dirtier it
was, the quicker they end. A war without cost of blood and treasure
is a war that would never end. Some countries had started changing their tactics and were using holograms to track down and kill
human civilians, or their enemy, to try and win victory. The idea of
using holograms as a means of 'saving' human life was having the
opposite effect. In wars, holograms were killing civilians wholesale,
because the countries had quickly learned that killing a hologram
exacted no cost on the enemy, and without cost, who would ever
stop fighting?

One of the most disturbing uses of the holograms were in
violent fantasies. People would create a hologram of a boss, an ex-
spouse, or someone they hated and, in the mild cases, yell at them a
lot. In the extreme cases, they would beat or kill the hologram, pay
the company for another, and do it all over again. As with any unhealthy activity, the more you do it, the more you are de-sensitized
to doing it. It doesn't matter if it's alcohol, drugs, sex, or violence.
The more you do it, the more extreme you have to go to get the
same excitement from it. The people that were indulging the violent
fantasy of hurting or killing someone they detested, kept getting
more extreme in their violence toward the holograms they would
kill, but eventually killing holograms wouldn't be enough to main-
tain the thrill level. Violence to humans was on the rise because in
the end there was nothing more thrilling to someone wanting to do
violence, then harming an actual person.

The only saving grace that Ben was able to build into his holograms was that they would never be able to develop their own
intelligence. He had feared that holograms with the ability to think
for themselves would eventually be a danger to humans, but he had
found out that his holograms had not needed the ability to think

for themselves to wreak havoc on the human race. Humans were using his holograms to wreak plenty of destruction without his holograms being able to think on their own.

Part 15

BEN WAS NOW APPROACHING his seventieth birthday. He and John continued to get together regularly and had become best friends. John had helped Ben get past and through so much over the years. The latest that Ben had difficulty with dealing was that one of his inventions had essentially struck a match to civilization and was burning it down before their eyes. John tried to reassure Ben that it was all in God's hands. Ben had gone through his difficulty in believing and wanting his holograms of Dee and his daughter to be real. It took him a few years, but he got past it, and the world would get past it as well. John would tell him that eventually, the world would settle into a rhythm, and learn how to live with the holograms as a part of their lives. Ben realized that John was correct and tried to not concentrate on all of the harm currently being done by their mis-use. Every large technology change in history resulted in mayhem for a time. The printing press led to large scale executions in country after country, as the people in charge felt threatened by it. The practice of medicine led to thousands if not millions of deaths, because those early physicians had no clue what they were actually doing. Automobiles and airplanes killed tens of thousands before safety laws were passed to make travel into something other than taking your life into your own hands. Early computers were as likely to kill humanity as save it, as governments allowed computers more and more control over military weaponry. As with all new technology, regulations and laws would eventually catch up, and people would learn how to use the holograms more safely. Ben could only hope that society learned how to live with them well, before it completely fell apart.

Over those last ten years, Ben and the Board of Directors continued to become more at odds with one another. Ben continued to push for his inventions to be used more responsibly, especially the holograms, while the Board kept preaching profit, profit, profit. The animosity between Ben and the Board eventually got to the point, that the Board fired Ben. Initially Ben was shocked by the firing, but the three months since they fired him had been the most peaceful months he had in years. It had been such a relief to be away from the Company. It seemed a lifetime ago when they hired him. It had been such an exciting time. That excitement had long passed, and all that was left in his heart for the Company was ashes and bitterness. Of course, being the lab geek at heart he had always been, there was no possible way he was going to stop inventing. Retirement was something he couldn't even imagine. What would he possibly do with himself other than wait to die? He made the decision that he still had things to do and things to invent in him so he purchased a building not too far away from the campus. The top floor, he had renovated into a living space, and he moved out of the campus apartment provided to him by the Company. He had asked, and he was very happy when Ann said yes to come and work for him. He really wasn't sure what she would do, since it was just the two of them, but she had been with him for decades, and he couldn't imagine working and not seeing her there. She was his first employee when the Company hired him all those decades ago. It just wouldn't have been the same for her to not be his first employee again.

For a time, all they did was talk, since there wasn't much to do until Ben thought of something he wanted to invent. Of course, there were the standard invitations for this interview or that appearance, so Ann politely declined every request that was presented. Their days consisted of sitting on a sofa that sat in the middle of a five thousand square foot floor of the building, talking for hours on end each day. There was nothing else on that floor, or the other four unoccupied floors either. For Ben's living quarters floor there wasn't much either. The apartment that the Company had provided was around two thousand square feet and Ben didn't even fill half of that, so a five thousand square foot space looked very spartan. Most days Ann arrived early and stayed late. They had known each other for nearly forty years and Ben learned more about Ann in the weeks since he was fired than he had ever known about her before. He had no clue that she had been married and that her husband died when she was thirty-five. Ben didn't even know that she had children, and that she had grandchildren. Ben was embarrassed to admit to her that he had not even known her age or her birthday, until she came to work with him here. He apologized to her for being so uninvolved. He spent decades so focused on his work, that he had missed so much going on around him. He had seen Ann hundreds of days a year for nearly forty years, but never once noticed what a kind and wonderful smile she had. When she laughed, her eyes would sparkle a bit, and if he got her laughing hard enough, she had the most adorable snort that she couldn't control at the end of her laugh. It had been three months since he was fired, and he had yet to think about doing any work. He found that he so enjoyed talking to Ann and just looking at her face, that work seemed very unimportant.

One day they were chatting about this or that and nothing in particular, when Ann made some large gesture with her hands and arms to describe something. As she brought her hands back down, her hand brushed Ben's hand. Rather than pull away, her hand lingered a bit, and they both looked at each other. Ann's cheeks flushed a bit, and Ben's hand moved to hold hers. They both smiled at each other. Ann leaned in and kissed Ben softly on the lips, and Ben kissed her back. The kiss was so gentle and sweet. Dee was the last woman Ben had kissed and that had been over forty years ago. Kissing Ann seemed so natural, and comfortable, as if they had been kissing each other their entire lives. After the kiss, they held each other. Both of them teared up a bit while they held each other. Ben was days away from being seventy years old and Ann was sixty-five, but it was as if they were both young again. Both of them had been alone for so long, and had never anticipated finding anyone so late in their lives. Ann had been keeping a secret for over twenty years about her feelings for Ben. She had loved him for a long time, but never acted on it because of his feelings for his dead wife. She didn't actually think Ben was capable of having feelings for anyone else but Dee, especially after he created the hologram of her. She had simply assumed that Ben would never be able to let go of his memories of her, but the last several years, she had seen Ben move past those memories, and finally let go of the past. She had been thrilled when the Company fired him and he had asked her to come with him. She leapt at the chance. Even if Ben never returned her feelings, she was ready to spend the rest of her life at his side, whether he ever loved her back or not. She felt like a schoolgirl, she was so excited that they kissed each other. She didn't know that she could feel this way after all of these years. As they broke the hug, Ben raised his hand to her cheek and brushed away a tear. He stared into her eyes, and felt something he hadn't felt in decades. He felt happy.

Part 16

BEN AND JOHN WERE going to be seeing each other on Friday, but Ben couldn't wait. He walked up to John's door and rang the doorbell. His wife, Cathy, answered the door. She invited Ben inside. John was walking past and saw Ben. He walked over and he and Ben shook hands. John invited Ben into the living room to sit and talk. John knew something had to have Ben worked up. Ben was a stickler for appointments and being exactly on time for things, so to show up three days early was very outside the routine for Ben. They sat and John saw something on Ben's face he had never seen before. Ben was smiling from ear to ear, and looked as if he was going to burst. John urged him to let out whatever was bubbling up and Ben blurted out, "Ann kissed me." Ben acted as if he was a teapot that had just let out a bunch of steam. John smiled and asked, "And?" Ben continued. "I kissed her back." Ben was just beaming. John couldn't help but smile. "I can't tell you how happy I am for you both." Ben kept talking. "Ever since I got fired, she's been working for me, but we haven't really done any work. We've just been talking and talking. Every day for months now. It has been the most wonderful time. And we've known each other for nearly forty years. It just seems so comfortable with her. The last time I felt like this was with Dee. She's just so easy to talk to. I look forward to seeing her every day. I haven't felt like this in so long." John interrupted him, because Ben was obviously not stopping any time soon and was going from one non-sequitur to another endlessly. "Ben. Do you love her?" Ben stopped, and considered for a moment and then smiled. "I do. Very much. I didn't know it was possible, but yes."

John smiled. "So, what do you want to do about it?" Ben straightened up a bit. "I'm going to ask her to marry me." John continued to smile. "If you were in your twenties I would say, give it some time. But none of us are getting any younger. And if you think anyone other than me is performing the ceremony, you can get that out of your head right away." They both laughed. Ben would never even think of anyone else performing the ceremony. The two men continued to chat about this or that for a couple of hours, and then Ben went home. He wanted the proposal to be perfect so he had a lot of work to do before Ann came to work in the morning.

The next morning Ann put the key in the lock at work and came in the door. When she entered music began to play. She was a huge fan of Dave Matthews and she was amazed at what she saw. She was at the back of a huge auditorium and the Dave Matthews band was on stage. The crowd was going nuts. It looked as if she was in a twenty thousand seat arena. A security person met her at the door and escorted her to the front row, where it was just her and Ben. When she got there, Dave Matthews extended a hand to her and indicated that she should join him on the stage. A security person took her around to the steps to get up on the stage, and she was singing and dancing with Dave Matthews while he performed. After one of his songs, Dave Matthews announced to the audience that someone there had something very important to ask her, and he wanted that someone to come up on stage. Ben walked up to the stage, and took both of Ann's hands in his. The arena became very quiet. The only voice that could be heard was Ben's. "Ann. You and I have known each other for over forty years." Ann began to cry because she realized what was coming. Ben continued. "But these past few months I feel as if I got to know you. The time before that, I saw you, but never really knew you. I took the fact that you were in my life entirely for granted. I've spent over forty years living in the past, and almost forty years not seeing the person that was right in front of me. I have missed far too many days of having such an amazing woman in my life, and I don't want to miss one more." Ben got down on one knee, and pulled out a small jewelry box. He opened it, to show a beautiful diamond ring. "Ann. Will you marry me?" Ann smiled through the tears and shook her head yes.

She was so happy. Ben stood and they both hugged and kissed. As they did, the arena, the people in it, and the Dave Matthews band vanished. After all, Ben only had one night to write the hologram and even he has his limits on how much he can do in a single night. Ann looked around at the now empty room and smiled. "You're getting even better at writing those programs. Ben smiled at her, "I made an improvement here and there."

That Saturday, Ben and Ann were married by John. Ann's children and grandchildren attended. They were all so happy for the bride and groom. They had all gotten to know Ben quite well over the last few months, and were happy to see their mother and grandmother this happy. After the festivities, Ben and Ann went back home to the top floor of Ben's building. They really had no desire to go anywhere for a honeymoon, so they spent the next week or so, doing what they had grown to enjoy the most. . .. . talking day and night to each other.

Part 16

THE CHAIRMAN OF THE Board was sitting in his office, chomping on one of his stubby, unlit cigars. He rose from the chair and walked over to the windows overlooking the analysis area. His office loomed about thirty feet higher than the analysis room floor and was fairly centered over the room. His office was glass on all sides so that he could observe the work being done. The glass was one way glass however, since no one needed to be observing him. He looked out over twenty-thousand square feet of computers and scientists, all working on data from the scan. He hated that his company and its fortunes were in the hands of these egg-heads. He preferred products over information. Something you could make, feel, put in a package, and actually show to someone. He despised making his fortune in 'information'. Granted, it had made him one of the wealthiest men on the planet, and his company was responsible for a great deal of the scientific breakthroughs of the modern era, but every egg-head he saw irritated him to the bone. Nothing had made him happier than getting rid of the biggest egg-head he had ever met, when he fired Ben a few months back. He had been beyond thrilled when he was able to take Ben's holograms away from him and launch it as a product over his objections. Who did that egg-head think he was trying to tell him what he could and couldn't do with his company? The head egg-head had finally created some-thing he could package as a product. There was no way he was listening to anything Ben had to say about it. Since the holograms, Ben hadn't come up with anything new. Good riddance to him. One less of them to have to see, and deal with each day. When this scan analysis was played out, and there was no more money to be wrung out of it, he couldn't wait for the day he could cut every last one of them loose. He had gotten so irritated by even the sight of them, that he had security clear any hallway he was going to walk down, just so he wouldn't have to see them smile at him, or say hello, or wish him a good day. He would point at each of them through his one-way glass and say, "Soon you'll be gone, and you, and you, and you. . . . .." And do that over and over again. My god how I despise you all, he thought to himself.

On his desk, he had gotten a report from one of his security officers. He sat down to read it, and chewed on his cigar extra heavily. Apparently, Ben recently purchased a multi-floor, factory/warehouse type building. He stewed and stewed, the longer he read the report. What was that ungrateful egg-head doing over there? He stood back up and began pacing the room with his hands clasped behind his back. "I made that ungrateful bastard." He said while pacing and staring at the floor. "Who the hell does that little egg-head think he is? He wouldn't have a penny to his name if it weren't for me. I made him a rich man." His pacing was getting quicker and angrier. "He pretends to be played out with no new ideas, leaves, and then decides he's got something more to do?" He was becoming furious. "No. No. No. I won't have it. That little egg-head is my property and if he's got anything left in his tank it belongs to me. If that little bastard thinks he can walk away from me and do something else, then I will enlighten him to the actual situation." He hit a button on his desk phone and told his assistant to have the head of the legal department to come to his office immediately and to bring any pertinent information regarding Ben's contract.

The attorney stepped into the Chairman's office and looked as nervous as every other person who has ever stepped into his office. The Chairman motioned for him to take a seat while chomping on his cigar. "I sent for you six minutes ago. With what I pay you, do you believe I deserve to be kept waiting?" The attorney shook his head no as if he was fearful of being smacked around a bit. "You will be prompt from this point forward or you will find employment elsewhere. Am I understood?" The attorney meekly replied, "Y-y-y-y-yes Sir" The Chairman sat down in his chair, leaned back, and turned the chair so that his back was to the attorney. "Now. What have you found in doctor Prentiss' contract? I know he is working on something and I want it." The attorney dreaded the answer he was about to give. "S-s-s-s-sir. There really is nothing we can do about that. Once Doctor Prentiss was terminated, anything he develops after that is his property." The attorney braced himself for the onslaught that was sure to come his way. Instead, there was nothing but silence. Somehow that scared him even more. The only word he received from the Chairman was, "Leave." The attorney wasted no time and got out of there as fast as he could. The Chairman had no intention of leaving it there. He called for his assistant. Once she entered the room, he turned his chair around. "Get me Bob."

Part 17

BEN AND ANN WERE sitting on the sofa in their living room. Ben was holding Ann, as she laid back into him. Ann squirmed a bit and said, "You know. Today is our one-month anniversary. I was thinking of what I want." Ben now squirmed a bit. He didn't know that he should have gotten a gift for a one-month anniversary. Ann continued, "I want you to pick out a song that will be my song." Ben perked up. He could definitely do that. Ann kept talking, "And I was thinking for your gift you could pick out something for me to wear tonight. Now Ben really perked up. He became as excited as a junior high school boy who just heard it was pizza day. He had an immediate response. "Sheer, see-through black wrap, robe, or whatever you call it." Ann turned around and chuckled. "You always want that. I'm sixty-five years old. Why do you always want me to wear something see-thru?" Ben smiled. "Because, you are the most beautiful woman in the world and clothing just does not do you justice." Ann gave him a kiss, "Good answer." She got up to go to the bedroom to change. Ben began searching through the songs on his system and found the perfect one for Ann. When she came back into the room, Ben became speechless. The sight of Ann always did that to him. Ann asked him if he found her song yet, and all Ben could do was to nod his head yes. He hit a button on a remote control and a song by Sade began to play. It was called 'No Ordinary Love.' Ann moved back to the sofa and sat next to him again. She listened to the words and began to cry. It was perfect. She loved the song and she loved him. They held each other and listened to the rest of the song. Ben then hit replay and stood up, inviting her to dance with him. She complied and they held each other, rocking back and forth to the music.

Part 18

BOB WALKED INTO THE office of the Chairman and took a seat. He never waited for an invitation to sit. He ran security for the Company, and had done enough of the Chairman's dirty jobs to earn the right to sit as he pleased. The Chairman offered him one of his cigar's, a sign of respect that the Chairman offered to no one else, as he had no respect for anyone else. Bob had been with him for over twenty-five years and had proven himself time and again as someone on whom the Chairman could rely. Bob took one of the cigars, cut the end with a cigar cutter, pulled out a lighter from his pocket, and warmed the cigar before lighting it. He always warmed the cigar before lighting, as anyone who enjoys a fine cigar does. The flavor just isn't the same if you light the cigar cold. He took the smoke into his mouth, held the flavor there for a moment and exhaled. The Chairman always had exceptional cigars, though Bob never knew why, since he had never seen the Chairman smoke one before. "Bob, I need you to do something for me off the books." Bob smiled. It seemed as if most of what he did for the Chairman was 'off the books.' "Name it," Bob said as he always did. "As you know doctor Prentiss was released some months ago. After his release he purchased a rather large factory, and I believe he is working on something new." The Chairman was chomping hard on his cigar as he walked around the room with his hands clasped behind his back. "I want to know what he's working on. By rights, any project he works on should be mine and I want it." Bob let out a large puff of cigar smoke and stood up from his chair. "Understood. I'll get right on it, Sir." With that Bob left the office. The Chairman smiled and was looking forward to Bob's success. In all of the time Bob worked for the Chairman, Bob never let him down. Whatever Ben was working on would soon be where it belonged, with the Company.

Bob met with some of the I.T. people at the Company who had done some, shall we say, less than legal things for him in the past. He used them because he could always count on their discretion and they were very good at what they did. Bob wanted them to hack into Ben's computers and pull off anything on which he may be working. The I.T. guys warned him against that. They reminded him that it was Ben who designed the malicious code that the hologram product department used to disable any computers that tried to get around the Company safeguards. The code that Ben had written was very thorough in destroying any computer that accessed the Company computers. They were sure that Ben probably had far worse code than he provided to the Company. Bob was insistent, but at least relented to the I.T. guys and allowed them to set up an independent system separate from the Company's computers, so that if Ben did have the malicious code, it would only fry the computers on the separate system, and not the entire Company's computer network. They nervously began their hack, and within seconds. The computers they were working on started going nuts. In less than one minute, every circuit in every computer on their separate network started throwing sparks. Small flames emerged from various parts of the machines, and the cables leading to the computers began to melt. Whatever Ben did, it was far worse than anything he had written for the Company. They had never seen the disabled computers catch fire and melt before. There would be no hacking of Ben's computer system. Bob would have to find another way of accessing the data the Chairman wanted.

Part 19

BEN AND ANN GOT home from doing a bit of grocery shopping. They enjoyed going together and picking out what they would cook that day for lunch and dinner. There was a beautiful little store down the street that had the best produce. Ben had never enjoyed shopping before. He always resorted to ordering something, or Ann would often bring him food over the time they had known each other. He was quite enjoying this new routine of going places with Ann. The enjoyment of the moment faded rather quickly though when they got inside. Ben's computer was alerting him to a problem. He sat down in front of one of the computers to see what was wrong. Apparently, someone had attempted to hack into his system. Ben smiled a bit imagining what a mess that they must be cleaning up right now. He ran a trace to see where the hack originated and found the code for his malicious code. It was asking him if it should continue and repel Ben's trace. Ben put in his backdoor code to tell it to stand down and let his trace proceed. The fact that his code was there meant that the Company had tried to hack him. Sure enough, when the trace was complete, the address was one of the offices of the I.T. department. They must have set-up an isolated system so as not to destroy the computers in the entire Company. Smart. The Company must think he's working on something. He thought maybe he should give them a goose to chase for fun. Ann was putting away the groceries, and Ben came into the kitchen to help. She had her Dave Matthews Band music playing. The next song came on, 'The Space Between.' Ben was only half listening to it, when something clicked in his head. He immediately stopped what he was doing. Ann was a bit concerned. Ben looked like a statue. He stood motionless for a good two minutes, and Ann was getting worried. All of a sudden, Ben grabbed her shoulders, pulled her close and gave her a big kiss. "That's it!," was all Ben said before rushing out of the kitchen and down the elevator to the bottom floor where his lab was located. The lab had not been used since he bought the building, since all he has done for months is talk to Ann. Ann was excited when Ben rushed out of the room. She had seen that look on his face before, though in the past it never came with a kiss. He had an idea for something and would now be spending endless hours working on it. Ben organized a bunch of whiteboards and began doing his favorite thing in the world, next to Ann. . . . . .math. Ann came down the elevator and told him she was going to go out and grab a couple of things she had forgotten for dinner, and that she would be right back. Ben mumbled an acknowledgment and she left the building.

Bob had put a back up plan into motion and had two of his men staked outside the building in which Ben and Ann lived and worked. They had not been there very long when they saw Ann come out of the building. They had instructions to pick up whichever one of them exited the building first. They followed Ann until she was a block away from the building and then parked in the street to block her path. They exited the car and opened a back door. Ann had a concerned look on her face and attempted to go around the car. The two men made it obvious that was not an option. They motioned for her to enter the car and no one said a word. Ann got into the car and they drove to a parking lot not far away. Ann recognized it immediately. They were at the Company. They escorted her inside, and then up to the office of the Chairman. One of the men pointed for her to sit in a chair and she complied. The two men took up positions at the door. The Chairman entered the office and he offered Ann something to drink. She declined and asked him why she was there. "Now Ann. You worked for me for several decades. I heard about your recent marriage to doctor Prentiss and simply wanted to offer my congratulations. Forgive me if it came across as being a bit heavy handed." Ann squirmed in her seat. She was terrified. The Chairman continued. "In light of your long length of service I wanted to give you a wedding gift." The Chairman moved directly in front of her, chomping on his cigar. Ann tried to look strong, but it was a failed attempt. She was shaking. "My gift to you, is that if you find out what your husband Ben is working on, I won't destroy the two of you." Ann was desperately trying to hold back the tears in her eyes, but a few escaped and streamed down her cheeks. "If Ben is willing to turn over whatever he is working on, he will get the same royalties as before and I will continue to make him a rich man. I would much prefer that we all be friends after all." The Chairman sat in his chair, leaned forward, and clasped his hands together on his desk. "You don't want us to be enemies after all, do you Ann?" Ann shook her head no in terror. The Chairman motioned for the two men to take Ann. They motioned for her to get out of her seat. They escorted her back to their car, and they dropped her off in front of the building she shared with Ben. Her hands were shaking so badly that she had difficulty putting in the entry code to get inside. When she did, she saw Ben working on his whiteboards. She screamed for him. Ben immediately turned around and saw that Ann was crying and in shock about something. He rushed to her to hold her and see what was wrong. Through a cracking, terrified voice, she told him everything that had happened. Ben was enraged.

Ben went to his lab to begin preparing a few things. He figured that the Chairman wasn't going to stop until he got what he wanted from Ben. He needed to make sure that he could protect Ann. She had been terrified by her encounter with the Chairman, and he never wanted to see that look on her face again. If the Chairman wanted something Ben was working on, he would make sure that he got it.

Bob left the Chairman's office with instructions to bring back something concrete regarding Ben's research. He grabbed his two reliable guys and they headed to Ben's building. They parked outside and waited for the building to go completely dark. They went to the door, disabled a surprisingly simple alarm, and entered the building. The door opened to a foyer, and through the foyer was Ben's lab. There were a few work benches, a few computers, and several whiteboards. One of the computers was active. Bob searched the hard drive and hit the jackpot. The file was name FTL, and it was a very large file. Bob plugged in a drive and copied the file contents to the portable drive. Once the copy was complete, they left the building. The next morning, Bob met with the Chairman. Bob showed him the portable drive and he inserted it into a laptop he had brought with him. On the screen came up schematics in the background. The foreground had a title come up that said FTL. It then faded and a longer title came up. Faster Than Light Drive. The Chairman was beside himself with excitement. Ben was working on an engine that could travel faster than light, and the Chairman was going to become even richer once they download these designs. Bob clicked the next file, and an animation came up. It was a small guy that looked like the Martian from the Bugs Bunny cartoons. It was walking toward a rocket. The Martian then pulled out a match, rubbed it on the side of the rocket to light the match. He then held the match to a fuse that led to the rocket. Once the fuse burned, the rocket took off, did several loops, and then crashed to the ground. From the explosion, the Martian was covered with soot, and a large animated word scrolled across the screen. . . . .'WHOOPS'. The laptop then began to make noises no computer should make. It sparked and crackled a few times, and then smoke came out of it. Ben's code had thoroughly fried the laptop. The Chairman chomped heavily on his cigar while he was seething, and marched over to Bob. "I want that research. I don't care what you have to do. I want it here and I want it now. Do you understand me. . .. . .. Bob?" Bob shook his head in acknowledgement and left the Chairman's office.

The next morning, Ben saw that three men had broken into his lab and stolen his 'research'. He began laughing to himself and wished he could have seen the look on the Chairman's face when he saw it. He knew the Chairman wasn't going to stop, so he made some additional preparations for their next attempt.

Bob was going to make sure that Ben understood the seriousness of the situation. He and his men waited outside Ben's building. He knew that every Friday night, Ben and Ann walked somewhere to go out to eat. They would escort Ben and Ann back to the Chairman's office, so that Ben could be made to understand the importance of turning his research over to the Company. Bob saw Ben and Ann exit their building and begin walking down the street. Bob and his guys got out of the car and began walking toward Ben and Ann. Ben and Ann stopped for a moment, and then resumed walking toward them. Once they got close enough to Ben and Ann, they motioned for them to get into the car. Ben and Ann complied and they drove away.

Ben and Ann were just finishing getting ready for their weekly date night. They both looked forward to getting out and talking to each other in a new setting. They especially had a lot to talk about with the Chairman breathing down their necks for Ben's latest project. They were going to go to a Mexican place Ann had always wanted to try. They left the building and Ben quickly noticed the three men approaching them. He reached in his pocket and hit a button. A hologram of Ben and Ann appeared ahead of them, dressed exactly as Ben and Ann were dressed.

The holograms resumed walking toward the three men. Ann whispered to Ben, "Won't two Ben's and two Ann's look a bit odd? Ben whispered back, there is a holographic shell around us. The shell mimics the surroundings, so for all intents and purposes, we're invisible as long as we don't move until they're gone." Ann smiled. She shouldn't be surprised by the things Ben could do, but she always was. "Won't they figure out that isn't us?" Ben nodded his head. "Once they are out of range of our grid the holograms will disappear. They aren't on the Company's hologram grid, so are only good as long as they are in range of me. In a few hundred yards, they will disappear." The three men and the holograms of Ben and Ann got into a car, and drove away. Once they were out of sight, Ben told Ann that they had better head back to the building.

Bob and his men were heading back to the Company with Ben and Ann. Bob was in the front seat on the passenger side and he was turned so that he could keep an eye on them both. One of his men was in the backseat with them, but he had no intention of relying on that. He wanted to make sure that they were delivered safe and sound to the Chairman. After a few blocks, however, there was an obvious issue. Ben and Ann began to blink out like a television with a lot of static coming through. After a few seconds of this, Ben and Ann disappeared. Bob turned back to face forward in his seat. In his head he was spewing curse word after curse word, but to anyone else he looked calm. The other men asked what he wanted them to do, and he told them to keep driving. Failing wasn't something Bob had ever done before, and Ben now accounted for both of the times Bob had failed. There wasn't going to be a third time. When Bob met with the Chairman, saying that the Chairman was not happy was the nicest way to describe the conversation. After an hour of the Chairman tearing Bob apart verbally, Bob finally won the day and got the Chairman to agree to leave Ben alone for a few months. With bringing in Ann, and making two attempts to steal Ben's project, Ben was obviously on high alert. Bob was confident that if they left Ben alone for a few months, Ben would let down his guard and they could make another attempt to steal the project. This would also give Bob ample time to plan a better attempt. He had considered Ben to be simply another lab geek. He underestimated Ben, and had no intention of doing that again.

Part 20

THE NEXT SIX MONTHS flew by. Ann had assumed a familiar role, in that she was making sure that Ben showered regularly, and ate when he should. It was far easier now that they were married to get him to listen to her on such matters. She also tempted him away from his work with more private inducements when she thought he needed a distraction from working his whiteboards nearly twenty-four hours a day. At the end of the six months, Ben simply sat in one of his chairs staring at all of the whiteboards surrounding him. Ann walked in and asked him what he was staring at so intently. Ben looked at her and said, "It's done. I can't believe it was so simple. I thought the math would take years." Ann looked at the boards and to her it just looked like board after board of gibberish. "What's done sweetheart?" Ben stood up, grabbed Ann in an embrace, and gave her a big kiss. Ben had obviously not brushed his teeth yet today and Ann marched him right to the bathroom to correct that error. Ben protested, saying that he needed to get to work on the equipment right away. Ann refused to capitulate and made him take a shower and put on fresh clothes as well. Once he was all fresh, Ben got right to work in his equipment lab, tinkering with this and that. None of it made any sense to Ann, but she knew how much Ben loved inventing things. She was sure that whatever doo dad he was working on, would be something the world would want even though it never knew it needed it. She smiled, gave him a hug from behind, and kissed his head before leaving him to tinker in his lab. Because of the former attempts to steal his project, Ben had moved his labs into the basement of the building. He and Ann lived on the fifth floor, and the other four floors were relatively unused. Now Ben believed the building was ready with his 'welcome to the building' program for anyone nosy enough to try and break in to commit any more mischief. He had also come up with a few surprises for when they needed to go out and about. He had to make sure that nothing could possibly happen to Ann, and he had no intention of letting his project fall into the hands of anyone else, especially the Company. The hologram technology got away from him and did damage to countless lives. There was no way this technology was going to get away from him. What he was working on would be far more catastrophic if it got into the wrong hands.

Ben needed to grab some supplies to begin working on the equipment for his current project. Ann wanted to come along, which Ben was glad to hear. He couldn't bear the thought of leaving her in the building alone and something happening to her. They made their way to the door and headed out for a day of gadget shopping.

Part 20

Bob and his team had waited for six months to try anything, hoping that Ben would have let his guard down by now. They had been watching the building for more than two days now, and not seen anyone come out. Bob's guys were constantly complaining about the food, the bathroom access, and the length of time they were spending cramped up in the car. Bob had gotten tired of telling them to shut up more than a day ago. Just then he saw Ben and Ann exit the building. They were holding hands and walking down the street as if nothing was an issue. Excellent, Bob thought to himself. Giving Ben time to let down his guard had worked. Bob and his team exited their car. Bob motioned for the men to split up, so that they could surround Ben and Ann. They were going to try and be a bit stealthier this time. They were getting close to the couple when one of his guys kicked a trash can on the sidewalk. Bob saw Ben look to where the noise originated. Bob yelled for his guys to grab them. As he did, Bob saw something he couldn't believe. Ben and Ann's were appearing all over the place. Every second or so another Ben and Ann was popping up. Bob and all of his men stopped running toward the couple because they couldn't tell which couple was the real couple. By now there were probably fifty Ben and Ann couples in the street with even more still coming. All of the couples were heading the same direction. They all turned the same, and acted the same. Bob thought that may allow him to track down the real couple. If they were all following the actions of the real Ben and Ann, then there had to be at least some lag between the actions of the real ones versus the copies. That hope was soon decimated though, when all of the Bob and Ann couples broke rank and started heading off in different directions. Some were walking, some were running, some were yelling for help, some were calm. It was chaos. Every couple was doing something different. Bob tried watching to see if one of the couples gave themselves away as the real thing, but he couldn't figure out which was which. He thought maybe the real ones would head back to the building, but none of the couples did that. He was at a complete loss. He messaged his men to head back to the car. With their cover blown, there was no point in continuing this pointless exercise. That was three times now that he had failed due to Ben. It was getting to be far more than irritating.

Ben and Ann arrived back at the building after a good day of gadget shopping. Ben had found everything he needed, that he didn't already have, and was ready to begin to work on assembly of the equipment. He hated to admit it to himself, but he was beginning to quite enjoy, his little duels with Bob. He just wished there wasn't a downside if Bob ended up coming out on the better end at some point. If there was no risk to Ann, he would relish their next encounter. It was like a live action version of chess, to see who could out maneuver the other. As he was unpacking the material, he had a sharp pain in his gut. It had been bothering him for quite some time, but it had always been something he could hide. Today's pain was something that had been obvious and Ann noticed it right away. She asked what was wrong, but Ben played it off as indigestion or something unimportant. Ann had no intention of letting it go. When Ben was with the Company, doctors were all over him all of the time, but since he was no longer with them, Ben hadn't seen a doctor since. Ann wasn't taking any chances, and she had no intention of taking a 'no' from Ben. Ben had hated all of the poking and prodding from the doctors over his decades with the Company, and had thoroughly enjoyed more than a year now of a doctor-free life. It was obvious that Ann wasn't going to let this go though, so he relented. Ben checked the surveillance equipment he had set up, not only around their building, but on all of the buildings in a three-block radius around their building. There was no Bob, and no obvious henchmen anywhere in the area. Ann had gotten Ben in right away with one of the doctors that had regularly probed, poked, and prodded Ben when he was with the Company. She trusted him, so they headed to his office. When they arrived, Ben changed into a one size fits no one gown and began grumbling to himself about being there. The doctor came into the exam room and made small talk, eventually asking Ben to describe any symptoms that he had been having. Getting Ben to relay symptoms was like trying to drag a chew toy away from your pet dog. Ben would give a single symptom, and Ann would nag him for another one until he relented. Finally, Ben shared everything that had been going on over the last several months. Ann was both scared and angry. Ben had been hiding a lot of things that weren't right with him. The doctor had the nurse come in to draw some blood for testing, and ordered some additional tests as well. Ann and Ben were there most of the day. The doctor had all the labs they needed on-site so thankfully got the results back quickly. Ann could see on the doctor's face that it was bad news. Ben had stage four pancreatic cancer. It was as close to a death sentence as a doctor could give. Ben's face was a blank, and Ann began crying as soon as the words came out of the doctor's mouth. The doctor told them the cancer was extremely aggressive. Without treatment, Ben could have a year, with treatment, they might be able to stretch that to two years. Ben told the doctor any treatment that would have an effect on his ability to think was off the table. Ann immediately got angry and told Ben that he would take any treatment that gave him even one more day. Ben refused, telling Ann that he had to finish his project before the end, and he needed a clear head to do it. They argued for a bit, but Ben had no intention of backing down. There was no way he was leaving this Earth without finishing this project. The doctor scheduled Ben for the various treatments that would give him as much time as he could get, and wished that he had better news as he offered his apologies. Ben and Ann headed back to their building, walking hand in hand the entire way back, saying nothing.

When they got back home, Ben held Ann's face in his hands and stared at her face as if he was drinking in every feature so that he could take it with him when the end came. For so long he thought he would never love anyone again. And now he couldn't imagine any possibility of loving anyone more than he loved Ann.

They held each other, Ann crying into his shirt. For some reason, Ben had not been upset by the diagnosis. He was at peace with it. Now he needed to make sure he completed his work before the cancer completed it's work.

The next morning, at breakfast, Ben and Ann agreed that they needed to tell John and Cathy. They were their best friends and they needed to know. Ben would also have to tell Tim, because they would need to make arrangements for the funding and operation of the 490 Foundation to continue after Ben was gone. Ann invited John and Cathy, and Tim and Lori over for dinner. Both couples said they would be there. When the couples arrived, they all had dinner, wonderful conversations, lots of things to laugh about, and then Ben shared the news with them. There were tears all around. By the end of the evening, everyone had hugged everyone. John and Tim prayed for Ben and Ann, and Ben told John and Tim that soon he would have something important to share with them, so be ready at the drop of a hat to come over. They said they would and everyone returned to their homes.

Part 21

THE CHAIRMAN HAD NEARLY chewed through his cigar he was so angry with Bob. "Three times Bob. Three times you let that. . . . . . . .egghead slip through your fingers." He walked over and stood directly in front of Bob and the chair in which Bob was sitting. The Chairman leaned over at the waist and put his face directly in front of Bob's face, but at an angle that made it obvious who was in charge. The Chairman was speaking so softly it was obvious he was seething with contempt. Small droplets of saliva dripped from the heavily chewed cigar and fell into Bob's lap. "Do I pay you to fail Bob?" Bob answered, "No sir." The Chairman continued, "You are correct Bob. So, the question is why are you failing Bob? And what exactly is Bob going to do to correct that failure?" Bob sat straight and looked ahead, just like he did in his days in the Army when a drill Sargent would stand in front of him, yelling in his face. "I expect you to succeed Bob. You are going to succeed, aren't you Bob?" Bob answered, "Yes sir" The Chairman stood up and walked back to stand behind his own chair. "I expect you to do whatever it takes to get me that information Bob. Do we understand each other?" Bob stood from his chair. "We do sir." With that Bob left the Chairman's office. He and his men would have to take a different approach. Grabbing Ben was obviously not working. They would have to break into the building and get the information. The real information this time. Bob knew the first time had been way too easy, yet he fell for it, and brought back a silly cartoon instead of the actual research data. This time would be different. He no longer underestimated Ben. He would need to prepare so that this time the mission would succeed.

Ben and Ann tried to make sure to spend as much time together as they could, even though Ben now had a timeline he could not affect in any way. Cancer was eating him alive, and it wasn't going to stop until it killed him. He had to complete his work before the cancer completed its work. He and the cancer were in a race, and he desperately wanted to win it. To ensure as much time together as possible, before the end, Ann began helping with Ben's work. She understood none of it, or what he was even trying to build, but she could make sure that he stayed fed, cared for, and could attach some thingamajig to a whatchamacallit when he needed her to do it. Over time, she actually got good at being his lab assistant, and she truly enjoyed her time with him. She tried not to think about how close they were to the end of their time together. It made her too sad, and she needed to be strong and happy for Ben. She was so thankful to God for the time they had together, and tried to not be so greedy about the time they wouldn't have once he was gone. She just focused on making as many of these memories as possible, before memories would be all that she had of him.

Two months had gone by since Ben had unleashed the Ben and Ann holograms on Bob to sneak away from him for a bit of gadget shopping. Ben had lost a considerable amount of weight and was looking more like a prisoner of war, than one of the world's richest men. It was a reminder to them both, that time catches up with us all, regardless of our earthly treasures. As Ben and Ann were working on some equipment, they heard noise coming from one of the surveillance monitors. As Ben went over to look, the power to the building flickered off and then back on again. Per Ben's design, the power to the upper five floors would appear to be off, but his 'welcome to the building' surprises would still be fully powered from the power source he had built when he first bought the building. He had his own hologram grid, and his own power for just such occasions. He went over to the monitors for the various floors, and set them to record. He didn't want to miss any of this. He asked Ann to pop some popcorn because a show was getting ready to start that she would not want to miss.

Bob brought four of his operatives to enter the building and retrieve the information the Chairman wanted. Each man would enter one floor, search the floor, and signal the others when the information had been found. Bob had researched the building, found the alarm permit, learned how best to disarm it, studied where the power entered the building, and how best to make the building go dark. They were all in position. When Bob gave the order, the power to the building was turned off, the alarm disabled, and each man entered his assigned floor.

Fifth Floor Man: He entered through a window on the fifth floor. As soon as his foot touched the floor, the floor changed into a wooden crow's nest like on an old pirate ship, where a lookout would stand. As he looked down, he seemed to be getting higher and higher above the water below. The sun was shining. There was a breeze, and he saw birds flying around. He looked around, but couldn't see any land anywhere. When he tried walking around the crow's nest, it swayed back and forth. He held on for dear life afraid to fall to the water below. It looked as if he were at least two hundred feet off the water. Every time a gust of wind would blow, it would send the crow's nest wobbling around. He closed his eyes and began to pray to survive, promising all kinds of things if he could just get out of this situation.

Fourth Floor Man: He entered through a window on the fourth floor. As soon as his foot touched the floor, it changed and became stone. There were stone walls all around him. Along the walls were torches, like you would see in the old treasure hunting movies. The stone, was damp, and he could hear the sounds of bats in the distance. He began walking through the cave, trying to find a way out, but it seemed endless.

Third Floor Man: He entered through a window on the third floor. As soon as his foot touched the floor, everything around him changed. He was on a train, barreling through the countryside at what appeared to be a high rate of speed. He started walking down the center aisle from car to car. He couldn't find anyone else on the train, and no matter how many cars he searched, the train cars seemed to go on forever. How was it possible that he hadn't gotten to the engine yet? He checked every sleeper cabin, every room, but there was no one. There had to be an engine up ahead somewhere, so he kept going forward.

Second Floor Man: He entered through a window on the second floor. As soon as his foot touched the floor, everything around him changed. He heard carnival noises and it appeared that he was in a fun house. There were mirrors around him that made him look short, fat, tall, etc. He heard clowns laughing, circus music, the sound of elephants and lions in the distance, and the honking of clown horns. He began to work his way though the Fun House, looking for an exit, but it seemed to go on forever. He could even smell popcorn and cotton candy. In some rooms, the floor would wobble, or move this way or that. In a couple of rooms, the perspective was altered, so that a door that looked far away, was actually a small door close to him. Some of the things made him a bit dizzy, but he was determined to find an exit.

First Floor Bob: Bob entered through a window in the first floor. As soon as his foot touched the floor, everything around him changed. He heard loud clanging, as four walls and a ceiling closed in around him. He had seen this kind of a room before. He was in a jail cell. To one side was a bench for sitting. He checked each of the walls and the bars. Everything appeared to be solid. There was no way out. Ben had gotten him again. Bob sat on the bench and shook his head. Ben could make holographic environments. That was a little tidbit he never shared with the Chairman. Well, Bob thought to himself. Nothing else to do, so he got comfortable. He laid down on the bench and waited for Ben to let him go. He assumed, his men were in similar situations on their respective floors, so there was nothing to do but sit tight and wait.

The men on all five floors heard a voice. It was deep, imposing, and ominous. It said, "Each of you will see a sign marked exit in your environment. If you touch the exit sign, you will be at the window you entered. If you exit, your evening will end and you will be free to go. If you stay, the environment you are in will turn from innocent and light-hearted to something more. . . . .intense." On each floor, an exit sign appeared. Each man reached out to touch it, and when they did, the window they entered became visible. Bob looked at his exit, and contemplated not touching it. He wondered exactly what Ben would do and how far he would go. He decided to not take the risk. He touched the exit sign, his window appeared, and he exited the building. As soon as he did, he saw his other men had exited their windows as well. Once they were all on the ground, the building lit up as a final 'screw you' from Ben, letting them know, that he had as much power as he needed for the building the entire time, and that their efforts had been pointless.

Ben re-set the system, and the normal security functions were back in place. He and Ann finished the last of their popcorn, after enjoying a wonderful show, put on by Bob and his crew. Ben had to admit to himself, that it was fun seeing his holographic environments in action. They had worked beautifully. But he knew, now that Bob had seen them, the Chairman would want them desperately. It would be yet one more thing Ben would have to keep out of his hands before the fast-approaching end.

Bob sat in the Chairman's office for yet another unpleasant meeting, to discuss his latest failure. Bob fully expected to not only be chewed up one side and then the other, but to be fired. Instead, the Chairman was quite calm. Somehow, that worried Bob even more. An angry Chairman was something to which he was accustomed. A calm one was unnerving. The Chairman never turned around to face Bob. "Bob, Ben has been a far worthier adversary than I ever dreamed. Some part of me has to respect that. But none of that matters at the moment. His holographic environments and whatever else he is working on will be mine soon. I just got a copy of his latest medical report. Ben is dying. He has a few months or a year at most. We may not be able to get his research from him, but getting it from his wife, after he's gone will be child's play." With that he dismissed Bob, and went back to chomping his cigar. Bob was divided. A part of him wanted to go after Ben until he finally won. The other part was glad to not risk racking up any more failures to him. With that he left. He would have a good deal of time to figure out how to wrest the research from Ann, after Ben's death.

Part 22

THE NEXT FEW MONTHS, Ben tried his best to finish his work before the end came. Ann had been such a blessing to him. He only wished he could have had more time with her. Ben was never one to be significantly overweight, but he was never a thin rail either. Before the diagnosis, he had been just under two hundred pounds, much of that thanks to Ann over the years, making sure that he ate regularly. Now he hovered over a piece of equipment, with a frame that was not even one hundred and thirty pounds anymore. The cancer was taking its toll day by day. Ann monitored his weight daily, but there was little she could do other than watch it decline day by day. Ben was weak, and had trouble doing everything, yet still he worked on day and night as best he could. Ann had found skills in this time that she never envisioned that she had. She had become the best assistant that Ben had ever had. She had gotten exceptional at soldering, welding, putting things together, and bringing Ben's designs to life. Even John and Tim had been coming over to help where and when they could. Not a one of them had a clue what any of it did, but they wanted to help the man that they had grown to love over the years. The day it was all complete, Ben had to write it on a board that they were ready. He was on oxygen, in a wheelchair, and had lost the ability to speak, due to how weak he had become. He asked Ann to have John, Tim, and their wives meet them in front of the building, so he could finally show them what they had helped him create.

The six of them stood in front of the building. It was a busy day, with cars going by, and people going in and out of shops and restaurants up and down the street. Ben motioned to Ann, and she hit play on her phone. Ben had recorded something for them all before he had lost his ability to speak. "My friends. I knew my voice was going, so I wanted to record this before it was completely gone. You all have been helping me over these last months to make something, even though you had no clue what it was. I cannot begin to thank you for your friendship and your love over the years I have known you all. I spent the majority of my life alone, and always thought it would be that way, but in you all I have found more love and friendship than one man could ever deserve. I wouldn't trade my life for anyone else's. To my dear Ann. I am so sorry it took me so many years to see the amazing woman right in front of me. If I have one regret, it's not marrying you far sooner, so that we could have had more time together. I never dreamed I could love anyone as much as I love you. Since I met John, I had always wondered how God did what he did. He can be everywhere, see everything, he knows the past, present, and future. He can direct our paths when he chooses, and cause things to happen or prevent them from happening, according to his plan for us. It wasn't until I heard one of Ann's songs from Dave Matthews, that the idea hit me. The song was called 'The Space Between.' Imagine the number 1 and the number 1.1. The difference between the two numbers seems so small, but between them is an infinite set of numbers. No matter how many decimal places you go out, there is always more that you can go. Since God has control over all time and space, I began to think about that reality in time. For us the time between one second and another is one second, but to God, who has all control over time, the space between one second and another is infinite. When you have infinite time between each second, the question becomes what can't you do? So, what would happen if we had the ability to slow down time? What would we see? What is there? Now, as you know, I have had no time to test this, so we are all going to see together if there is anything between the seconds. If you're ready, let me know, and then Ann will hand each of you a remote that will keep you in our little time bubble. She will then hit the button, which will trigger the device you have all helped me build." There wasn't a one that didn't say yes. Ann handed each of them their remote. She then reached over, and hit the button, triggering the device. At first nothing happened, but then the bubble around them all began to waver and shimmer a bit. The world around them began to move more slowly. As their surroundings continued to slow, it appeared that everyone was coming to a complete stop. Of course, time was still passing, so they weren't actually completely stopped, but time was passing so slowly, none of them could perceive that anyone was actually moving. As their surroundings were slowing to a perceived stop, other things began to appear that were moving at what they perceived to be a normal speed. Once everything appeared to be stopped, these other things came into focus. They were beings of what they could only imagine was pure energy. They looked like people, but were shimmering and moving from place to place without walking. There were hundreds of them. It was as if they were floating from one location to another. Each of these beings seemed to be following a specific person, as if each was assigned a specific person. It looked as if they would whisper in the person's ear, or guide them this way or that. One of them looked toward Ben's group and floated over their way. It seemed to look at them with great curiosity. It moved inside of their bubble of time and moved a glowing hand along each of their faces, while tilting its head as it cupped the cheeks of each of them in turn. As it did this, each of the people in Ben's group felt an overwhelming sense of being loved and cared for by the being. After touching each person, the being floated away, and up toward the sky. After the being was out of sight, they heard a deep, booming voice coming from above, "It was all for you." After that, the time bubble began to waver and shimmer, as the time around them began to speed back up. In short order, they were back in the normal flow of time. All of them walked back into the building, speechless over what they had seen. They all sat down, trying to put into words what they had seen. John was the first to speak. Tears were flowing down his face. "Ben, I can't even begin to thank you enough for this. I don't know what to say other than, I've seen angels today." All of them were crying tears of joy over what they had just experienced. Ben motioned for Ann to hit the button for his second recording. She did, and again they listened to Ben's voice. "If everything worked and went according to plan, my guess is that we saw a few of God's angels and how they intervene in our lives to guide us, direct us, and protect us according to God's will for our lives. I have wanted to tell you all so long about what I've been working on and what you've been helping me to build. I've thought about this for so long, after the scan was complete and showed that we were all alone here, on this little blue ball moving through the vastness of space. For a time that depressed me to no end. But after meeting John, and through him, getting to know Christ, I came to look at it as an amazing gift. God gave us these incredible minds, that have taken us from the wilderness into the modern world. We have the ability to create and imagine the most amazing things, but we bore easily. We always need a challenge, the next puzzle to solve. God made us this way, so what was he to do with a creation that always needed another puzzle? He created a vast universe with limitless puzzles out there to solve. If the human race lives for billions of more years, there will still be more puzzles to solve and keep us occupied, and each one allowing us to appreciate more and more what he created for us. As my quest to solve the next puzzle comes to an end, I can't wait to look down from heaven and watch, as the next puzzles get solved. Now for a bit of bookkeeping. This technology cannot exist. If anyone got their hands on it, I can't even begin to imagine the devastation that could be caused. Ann will type the word 'Chairman' into one of the computers. My security program will then destroy every computer and piece of technology connected to them. What I will need you all to do, is to help Ann then dispose of all of the computers and the technology. My holographic environment technology, and the time slowing technology, must all be destroyed. I bought a grinder that can grind up all of the computers, notes, and tech into very tiny, useless pieces. Everything has to go into it. I wish I had more time with you all. You are the best friends anyone could ever have, and Ann, you are the love of my life. Every day with you has been a gift from God, and I couldn't be more thankful to him for you." With that the recording ended. Ann went over and typed 'Chairman' into a computer. Every electronic item in the entire building began to spark, and was destroyed. After the flames had subsided and the machines had cooled, they each began to haul every piece of hardware, and all of Ben's records into the room with the grinder. It was as large as a car, and it made quick work of everything they threw into it. In rolling bins underneath, all of the dust size pieces were collected. Once it was all done, they gathered in the kitchen, and had one last meal together. They all shared the most wonderful stories of their past times together, and laughed and ate for hours. Ben was having a particularly difficult time by the end of their time together. John lifted him from his wheelchair, and carried him to his bed. Surrounded by his friends, and holding the hand of the wife he loved, Ben slipped peacefully away and into the hands of God. Ann kissed his hand, and his cheek as she cried. His friends cried as well, as they said goodbye to a man that had become so dear to them.

Part 23

BEN HAD DONE HIS best in the lead-up to his death, to make things as easy as possible for Ann and his friends. He had planned a small ceremony after his cremation for Ann and his friends to give their final good-byes as they scattered his ashes. There was a lake that he and Ann would go to get away from civilization for a couple of hours now and then after they got married. They liked it so much, that they had bought the lake for their own, private getaway. Ben's ashes would be scattered there, at the shore in front of their little one-bedroom cabin. Ben had already transferred every asset he owned in the world to Ann prior to his death, so that nothing would be tied up for any length of time after he died. He had also transferred money to each of Ann's children and grandchildren so that they would be taken care of and Ann would know that they were all secure throughout their lives. The children and grandchildren would receive monthly income from trusts in each of their names for as long as they lived, and as more grandchildren or great-grandchildren were born additional trusts would be set-up or existing trusts transferred as children or grandchildren died. As Ann had requested, a trust was established for her, and she had insisted that the 490 Foundation receive the revenue from Ben's royalties and ownership of his stock in the Company. She had seen the attention spotlight that being a billionaire put on Ben and she wanted no part of it.

Ben had also arranged for a delivery and recording to be delivered to the Chairman upon his death. Movers had come to pick it up the day after Ben's death, and they delivered it to the office of the

Chairman as Ben had paid them handsomely to do. They handed a portable drive to the Chairman, along with several crates. The Chairman opened each of the crates and all of them contained what looked like dust and bits of plastic, wires, and metal. He put the drive into a computer and saw a very weak Ben. "Chairman," Ben said in a very weak voice. "In these crates are the remnants of every computer, electronic device, whiteboard, and piece of paper that I owned. The only electronic items I have left in the world, are portable drives containing footage of every kidnap attempt, attempted break-in, financial records of every illegal trade, take-over, blackmail, bribes, acts of violence, intimidation threats, phone recordings, and hundreds of other illegal and shady things you have done over the years. I have never trusted you, and for good reason. I built traps into every computer and electronic device you have ever used at this company, and it is all sitting in the offices of lawyers all over the world with one instruction. If anything happens to my wife, my friends, or their families that appears the least bit unusual, those documents are to be turned over to their local authorities for prosecution." Ben leaned into the camera for emphasis. "I have no more inventions for you, so keep your hands off of my friends and my family, or I can promise you, that you will spend your remaining years in prison, or at the very least destitute from the litigation and the lawsuits that will come." Ben then leaned back in his chair and put his oxygen tube back in as he struggled to breathe. 'This egghead made you rich beyond your dreams. Be satisfied with it and move on, or else." The video ended. The Chairman sat in his chair chomping his cigar. He wasn't sure whether or not he should be furious, or impressed. Ben had not been the typical egghead. He had proven himself to be a formidable adversary and the Chairman had not expected that. He told his assistant to get Bob on the line. Bob called in and the Chairman answered, "Bob. Scrub any plans to retrieve anything from Ben's wife. Ben destroyed all of his work before he died." He paused while Bob spoke. "I have it from a reliable source. There is nothing left to get. Don't bother his wife, his family, or his friends." With that the Chairman sat back for a moment thinking. After a couple of minutes, he leaned back forward and got about the business of the day, first telling his assistant to get all of the crates out of his office.

John, Tim, and their wives had hardly left Ann's side since Ben's death, except to go home to sleep. Over the three days since he had died, they all sat around telling stories of their times with Ben. They laughed, they cried, they hugged, over and over again about their friend, and the man they all loved dearly. He had been cremated, and the urn holding his ashes was in their living room. In a few days, they would go to their lake and scatter his ashes, as he had wished. As the five of them were sitting around and talking, Ann's phone rang. It was the funeral home. Apparently, they had been flooded with e-mails, phone calls, text messages, and messages on social media. Thousands of people, from all over the Country were making plans to come to the memorial. The funeral home called to inform her that there was no possible way to hold the service at their facility. Since Ann had rented such a small room, the crowd would interfere with the other services being held, not to mention clog the streets around their site. Ann thanked them and hung up. She told her friends what she was told and John had an idea. He told Ann if she were up to the cost involved, he would like to take care of the arrangements. She was so relieved for John's help, and she didn't care what it cost. The man she loved was worth every penny. John and Cathy got up to leave, and asked Tim and Lori for their help. The four of them left to make arrangements. Ann got up to grab Ben's urn, returned to the sofa, and held it tight against her chest.

Ben's memorial service would be in four days. There was little time to waste, so Ben's four dearest friends got to work. Tim and Lori took care of social media, and communication with everyone wishing to attend. Ben's memorial would be like the 490 Foundation. No one would be turned away. John and Cathy worked on the venue. At first, they thought a local High School gym, but the people looking to attend outgrew that within hours. With as many people as had given notice of attending, even the professional basketball arena wasn't going to be big enough. Thankfully, the owner of the professional football team in town, had known Ben and owed him a favor. John could think of no better time to collect. The owner showed them the open dates for the coming seven days and John and Cathy picked the one closest to the memorial date that Ann had set.

The next several days went by quickly. Ann was so thankful for their friends being so attentive to her these last few days without Ben. Living the remainder of her life without him was going to be beyond difficult. She had loved him for so long, yet even though she had imagined being his wife for years, the reality of being his wife had been so much better. He had been such a gentle, caring man. He had been alone and lonely for decades, but she couldn't think of a single time when her happiness wasn't more important to him than anything else in his world. Now that he was gone, she finally understood his need to make the hologram of Dee all those years ago. If she had his ability, the temptation to make one of Ben would be overwhelming. Thankfully, the commercial grade holograms available today were nowhere near what Ben was able to create, so for her, that would be a temptation she would never have to wrestle with in her remaining time on this Earth. She had always feared death, but now that Ben was gone, she found that fear gone. She wasn't looking forward to dying someday, but the thought of seeing her Ben again, made the idea of death more reassuring than scary. As she began to get dressed for the memorial, she put her see-thru black gown on, with nothing underneath of course. Just the way Ben liked it. She looked at herself in the mirror. She never understood what Ben saw when he looked at her like this, but she was so happy he saw her as a sexy and exciting woman. What she would give to see him look at her like that again. She sighed for a moment, and then changed into the dress she would wear to the memorial. She knew they couldn't hold it at the funeral home, but had no clue where her friends had moved it. They had kept very quiet about their plans.

They picked Ann up outside her building, and they began to drive. The ride was a quiet one. It was a very somber day. They would be saying goodbye to Ben in a very public way, and it would be as if that when they left the memorial service, they would be moving on to their lives where Ben would no longer exist. Thankfully, they all were filled with wonderful memories, that they would always cherish. They drove past hotel after hotel, where Ann was sure they would be having the memorial, but they kept driving. They got deeper into downtown, and she couldn't imagine where they were going. Then she saw the professional football stadium, and the marquee was scrolling the information for Ben's memorial. Ann began to cry. It was sweet of their friends to go to the trouble of arranging such a large venue, but she and Ben had been such homebodies. She couldn't imagine more than a few dozen people showing up, and a crowd that small would look lost in such a large arena. They drove into one of the underground parking gates, and John showed them their pass. They were directed to a VIP section of the underground parking, where they all got out of the car. They walked to the VIP elevator nearby and headed up to the field level. Security escorted them to where the stage had been set up in one of the endzones. As they cleared the field entrance, they were greeted by a packed arena of people cheering. Ann immediately put her hands to her mouth and began to cry. The arena held nearly seventy thousand people and she couldn't see an empty seat anywhere. How did so many people know Ben, or care enough about him to show up like this? John put his arm around Ann and hugged her close. "You and Ben have touched far more people than you know."

John showed her to her seat on the stage. The rest of her friends sat in their designated chairs on the stage as well. All except John. He walked within a few feet of the lectern at the front of the stage. On the large screens around the stadium were photos of Ben from his life. Some of Ann and Ben together were scattered in there as well. The photos of Ben ranged from when he was a child, up until a few weeks before he got really weak. There was beautiful Christian music playing in the background, that went perfectly with the photos. The photos dissolved one into the next. It seemed as if there were hundreds of them. Ann smiled when she saw pictures of Ben working, or doing something silly. She couldn't help but cry when she saw the pictures of their wedding. She missed him so terribly. As the noise of the crowd died down, John stepped up to the lectern to speak. As he did, the crowd sat down, and the music quieted, but it kept playing as the pictures continued. Even John got a bit choked up, and wiped a tear that formed in the corner of his eye.

"I want to thank everyone for coming here today to celebrate the life of a man that I was privileged and happy to call my friend. I would venture to say that none of you here today ever met Ben.

It may surprise you, that as famous as Ben was around the world, until the last decade plus of his life he was a terribly lonely man. He lost his family when he was a child, and having no relatives, was put into one foster house after another, largely ignored by the adults charged with his care. In elementary through high school, he was bullied, ignored, ridiculed, and treated as if he didn't exist by his classmates. In those lonely years of his childhood, he turned to books for comfort. He had a mind that got him into trouble with more than one teacher, even well into college. He usually knew more about the subject being taught than his teachers, and most didn't like that one bit. It was a rare teacher that encouraged his love of knowledge. Most would become irritated at being corrected by one of their students. Ben surpassed anyone that tried to teach him his entire school career, and with his accomplishments as an adult, it became clear to the world how ahead of his time Ben was. Most of our modern world today, is thanks to Ben. His greatest ac-complishment though he considered his greatest failure. When the scan showed that we were the only planet in our galaxy with intel-ligent life, Ben was devastated. You see, this terribly lonely man, was hoping that there was other life out there somewhere. But instead, he discovered that we were a planet as lonely as he was. In college, he met his first wife, Deanna. Deanna was pregnant when she went into early labor. She and the baby died, and Ben was left alone yet again. He did, what many of us do when things go wrong in our life and he blamed God. It wasn't until many years later, when Ben wandered into our Church, and this lonely man turned his life over to Christ, that he discovered that he was never actually alone. When we are at our lowest, and we feel as if we don't have a friend in the world, Jesus is there to be our friend and our comfort. He can be the shoulder we need to cry on, and the friend we need to listen to our problems. In the Bible, Jesus called us friends. There is no greater thing you can call another person than calling them your friend, and Jesus calls us his friends. Something amazing happened after Ben accepted Christ into his life. He and I became friends, and a better friend than Ben is hard to find. Then Ben met Pastor Tim, which most of you know, since he leads the 490 Foundation that Ben created. Then he met our wives and he was up to four friends.

Then a miraculous thing happened. His eyes were opened and the woman with whom he had worked for decades, became his friend and eventually his wife. I would like to introduce Ben's wife Ann." Ann stood up and gave a reluctant wave, trying not to burst into tears again, though the effort was proving to be useless. She sat back down and John continued. "This man who spent most of his life alone and lonely, was going into his twilight years with a life full of friendships, and a wife whom he adored and loved, and I know adored and loved him. If you will indulge me for a moment, I would like everyone who is a student at a Trade School thanks to the 490 Foundation, or graduated from a Trade School, and is now out in the world working and supporting yourself and your family, thanks to the 490 Foundation to stand." Across the stadium people began standing. From what Ann could tell, it was at least forty thousand of the people in the stadium. Before, they had all been numbers on a page, but to see so many of them here like this was amazing. "If you will remain standing, I would now like the people impacted by the 490 Foundation to stand. You would be married to, dating, or a child of a person that the 490 Foundation put through Trade School and helped to get a job." Every last person in the stadium was standing. Ann couldn't help but cry again. She covered her mouth with her hands as she cried. So many people impacted by her Ben. John continued. "This once lonely man, who thought he was completely alone in the world and the galaxy found something amazing in his life after he turned it over to Christ. He found that one person can change the world, not by inventing new technologies, but by helping one person. By changing the life of one person, you touch God. Ben touched so many people. People that he never met, and would never meet. But even after death, Ben will continue to reach out a hand and help someone in need. Some of you may notice that Ben doesn't send anyone to college, only Trade Schools. Ben was generally a quiet man that kept to himself, but one of the few topics that would get him going was how useless our university system has become. He never shied away from sharing his low opinion of a college degree. On the other hand, he had a high regard for people who could 'do' things. When he formed the 490 Foundation, he only presented Pastor Tim with two requirements. One was that the scholarships and support was only for Trade Schools, because he valued people who could do things more than he valued a college degree. Two, was that we never kick anyone out of the program. Ben believed in the forgiveness of Jesus. Jesus, when asked how many times should we forgive someone, said seventy times seven, which if you're good at math equals four hundred and ninety, or 490. If someone entered the 490 Foundation program and slid back into drugs, or whatever thing in their life had held sway over their past, we were to help them back, and stick with them, the way God sticks with us. It was our job and our mission to keep helping, as long as they needed help. Even if it's years after a student graduates, gets a job, and slides back into trouble, the 490 Foundation stands with them, just like Jesus stands with his friends, and you are all his friends. A story I told Ben once, and he seemed to really like, was that after Jesus was crucified, the eleven remaining Apostles were terrified that they were next, but after seeing Jesus again, once he rose from the grave they were inspired and driven. They all met in the upper room and when they emerged, those eleven changed the World. Ben was one man, and he changed the world. Today, here in this stadium, we are over seventy thousand. When we step out of this stadium and into the world, how will we change it for the better? Please rise, as we pray." Everyone in the stadium stood and John offered a prayer to the crowd. After it was over people began to leave. Ann hugged John tight and thanked him over and over, commenting on what a beautiful service it was. She hugged and thanked, Tim, Cathy, and Lori for being such good friends and working so hard on putting this together so quickly. Ann was moved beyond belief at the out-pouring of love from so many people. She was so happy that the Foundation would have all the money it needed to operate far into the future. Security escorted them out, and to their car. They returned Ann to their building. Soon she would be moving to a much smaller home, and turning the building over to the Foundation. As she walked though the building alone, she touched everything, bringing back a memory of Ben as she touched each item or piece of furniture. Some of the things she would clutch to her chest, as a special memory would grip her. She missed Ben so much. She laid in their bed, staring at a photo of them together. A tear streamed down her cheek. She kissed the photo, and said to him, "I love you sweetheart. I know you're in a wonderful place where you'll never be alone again. I'll be seeing you soon my dearest love." With that Ann went to sleep, and dreamed of Ben.

A Very Special Thanks...

To TC for all the work you did to help me write, and edit, and edit, and edit this book; WHEW!! We did it!

To my mother Joyce who helped in partial financing; Thanks Mom.

To Mrs. Dunn whose son Andy has cancer; You knew me for less than 2 hours. You listened to my story about having my VA and state benefits cut off after being injured on active duty in the military. You gave me some money to help with this book when no one else in America would. You gave 2 mites when everyone else was just patting me on the back for serving my country. You'll get back to Heaven before any of us will. My prayers are with Andy often. May the Father bless you and your family. www.caringbridge.org/visit/andydunn

To my good buddy Gigi with CrindelStar; You were the spark that started this fire.
Let's burn up the world with kindness. Thank you, darling.

To my new friend Kenny; Your last minute help is very much appreciated. Good Karma to you.

INTRODUCTION

This book's stories were taken mainly from a dream journal. Some of its contents were the work of the imagination of its writer. In no way were its contents taken from any other book, movie, play, idea, script, or overheard conversation, etc. If I have offended anyone, get over it. It's my very first book. As a disabled Vet, injured on active duty here in the states, I found there weren't too many people standing in line to help me get this book published, or to help with VA benefits that were cut off, Social Security benefits, or any other benefit that Vets are supposed to have. I sincerely hope that this book will open a door that, in the future, will help all the Disabled United States Veterans I have met. Good luck my brothers and sisters-n-arms. Help is on the way.

FORWARD

A few religions and cultures have, in some way or another, studied or have some insight to what dreams are about. Most just pass them off with the simple explanation of "the mind processing daily information". In a small way, this is true, to a point. However, dreams are much, much more. Take it from someone who survived a Near-Death-Experience, they are very real. The reasoning is easy and simple to understand. The body and mind have to rest from the physical and thought process. Our true being, the Soul, does not age, get tired, wear out, or die. It has always existed and always will. When the ego (conscious thought) is "asleep", the Soul is free to wonder the universal planes of existence. It can be in 50 different places at the same exact moment. Our problems that we have created here in the physical realm do not mean a thing to the Soul itself. What really matters most here is how we selfishly and selflessly use our energy to help others. Your Body Does Not Have A Soul. YOUR SOUL HAS A BODY! Use it wisely.

Your Soul's experiences, on the other realms and in other times, are transmitted to our conscience thoughts thru what we call a "Dream Memory". This memory descends from the Soul conscience, to the unconscious, to our thought conscience. By the time it reaches our thought process, it is translated to human life-and-experience-understanding.

Study your dreams, please. They will give you insight to what's going on in your life. Keep a Dream Journal, if only for a short time. There is room in the back of this book to record about a week's worth of dreams, depending on the length of your journeys.

Every once in a while, you will even meet people in your dreams before you meet them in person. Deja' vu is just the conscious mind making a connection with an unconscious memory. When you start recording your dreams, things in your life will start to change that no one else will ever notice, except you. You will begin to feel smarter around people who are oblivious to their own actions and surroundings in this physical existence. You will notice things that you would normally be oblivious to. There are miracles right in front of our faces every single moment of existence. We cannot see them because we are blind to anything but our own thoughts, emotions, and desires. Look, reach, study, and find your dreams' meanings.

This is about the way the 'Dream Study Process' works. The mind is like an onion. It is dozens of layers thick. We normally use 7 to 9 layers in our every day walk of life. Our dream memories are about 10 to 12 layers in toward the higher consciousness. When we remember and record our dreams, we invite the higher 10 to 12 layer consciousness into our everyday 7 to 9 layer understanding. When this happens, we get a higher understanding of existence because of the higher conscious intervention. Understand? We make ourselves smarter by realizing the higher consciousness in us. I started keeping a dream journal, off and on, in late '92. I realized, going through my journals years later, that some dreams are continual. I found some dreams are weeks and months apart. Study yours and see what you find. I hope you like these stories that came from my journal.

Good Journey,

Uncle Billy